RUADRI

Immortal Highlander, Clan Skaraven Book 3

HAZEL HUNTER

HH ONLINE

Hazel loves hearing from readers!
You can contact her at the links below.

Website: hazelhunter.com

Facebook:
business.facebook.com/HazelHunterAuthor

Newsletter: HazelHunter.com/news

I send newsletters with details on new releases,
special offers, and other bits of news related to
my writing. You can sign up here!

Chapter One

STANDING ALONE IN the medieval highland forest, Emeline McAra didn't see snow drifts. Somehow winter had transformed the world into a bridal boutique stuffed with wedding dresses. Dozens of them surrounded her, all big, beautiful confections of white satin and lace waiting to be donned and admired. Ice and frost became ruffled hems, beaded trains, and crystal-sequined headpieces. Beyond the gowns the river had frozen into an ivory carpet of sparkling light, down which wand-thin beauties might solemnly saunter as they modeled the latest gown trends: off-the-shoulder bodices, plunging V-necks, side cutouts, and statement sleeves.

Winter, Emeline decided, hated her.

"Healer McAra?"

Emeline might ignore the dark beauty of Shaman Ruadri Skaraven's impossibly deep voice, but she couldn't escape his presence—or the emotions he brought with him. Even before Emeline became a nurse she could sense other people's feelings, probably from the years she'd spent caring for her taciturn elderly parents. Since being taken with four other women to fourteenth-century Scotland, the dial on her gift had been turned up to full blast.

Time traveling had turned Emeline's natural, gentle empathy into a nightmare.

Since she'd arrived in the Middle Ages, the emotions of others came to her in a synesthetic jumble of colors, textures, sounds and scents. Depending on who projected the feelings, their anger could be a bright red hammer pounding inside her head, or an icy black torrent drenching her skin. Another person's worry enveloped her in a too-small straitjacket of stifling, damp wool. Fear tasted metallic and sharp, like licking a honed knife, while pain smelled of the aftermath of such a foolish act: tears and blood.

During Emeline's first week as a prisoner of the mad druids and their bizarre inhuman guards, the bombardment had never let up. Every time one of the other four women panicked, Emeline had been jolted and pummeled and smothered by their terror. Their situation had grown so desperate that the cacophony of fear from the others had made her constantly retch. She'd only just learned how to block the worst of the sensory attacks to protect herself, but she first had to be prepared for them.

Emeline had never been ready for anything about this man. To look at him wrenched at her heart, just as it had the very first moment he'd walked out of the shadows last night.

"Do you want for something?" Ruadri asked from behind her.

That question almost made her laugh out loud. How she wanted for something—so many things. To be held, comforted, and loved. To know if she would survive this insanity. To discover what it was like to be kissed.

To tell him that she had never believed in love at first sight.

To punch the shaman square in the nose for making her a believer.

"No, thank you," she said.

The words hurt her tight throat as she built the blockade in her mind to keep out his emotions, while keeping a tight grip on her own.

Emeline had no intention of making a ninny of herself, so she went back to her memory of the bridal shop in Inverness. All the magnificent, snowy gowns there had resembled an army of delicate, unsullied confection. They seemed silently smug, too, as if they knew she'd never have a reason to wear any of them. The mist around her combined with the pale sunlight glittering on the tree branches to become veils adorned with crystals and silk flowers, also forever out of her reach. The air in the shop had smelled of roses, but here every breath was so cold and clean, so pure. Almost too beautiful for her to breathe.

"But why can't you try on the bloody dress?" Meribeth Campbell demanded from her memory of that last day in the twenty-first century. As always, her gleaming blonde curls had lovingly framed Meri's pretty face, even when it went rosy with temper. "The blue is perfect for you. I even got the high neckline you fancied. Really, Em, there's nothing wrong with it. You'll look lovely."

"I ordered a size eighteen, Meri," Emeline said, eyeing the sapphire bridesmaid's dress brought in for her fitting. Judging by the dimensions, she might be able to squeeze one leg or arm into it, if she first starved for another month and then buttered herself. "I think they missed a digit."

The shop clerk checked the tag and grimaced. "It *is* a size eight, Miss."

"Of course, it is," Meribeth said, throwing her hands in the air. "How long until you can get the right size?" She scowled as the clerk went to consult with the seamstress who was waiting to do any needed alterations. "I can't believe this. My bloody wedding is next week."

This might be her last chance to get out of making a spectacle of herself, Emeline thought.

"You have four other bridesmaids, Meri. You'll not need me."

"What I need is... Oh, damn, I know what happened." She retrieved her mobile and pressed some buttons. "Lauren, it's me. Did Bride's Blush deliver your gown? What size is it? Och, the wallapers. No, don't send it back, it's Emmy's. She's yours here." She dropped her voice to a fierce whisper. "No, she hasn't tried it on, you goose. How could she?"

Meri didn't have to say it was half Emeline's size. Everyone knew how fat she was. Especially their coworker Lauren Reid, who dropped sly digs about her weight when-ever she could. Ironically Emeline had been on a strict diet for the last eight weeks in order to slim down enough to get into an off-the-rack dress. No one had noticed, not even Meri. Still, as her best friend and worst enemy nattered on, Emeline kept her forced smile firmly riveted in place. So what if she was black affronted by two reed-thin women who'd never know what deliberate starvation was like? She had to stop making this about her. It was all for Meri.

Emeline reached up with a trembling hand

to grasp the cross she no longer wore, her fingers curling against her sternum.

"Healer McAra," Ruadri said as he came closer, the snow crunching under his boots. "Does your chest pain you?"

Tears burned in Emeline's eyes as she was yanked back to the present—or the past—or whenever she was.

"No," she said, her voice unsteady. "I used to have a necklace…" When she realized her hand had curled into a fist, she dropped it to her side.

"Havenae you yet slept?" the shaman asked her.

"I'm no' tired."

And now she was lying. She'd tried to sleep, but the pain of her side wound and ankle combined with thoughts of him had made it impossible. She should tell him that since coming here last night she'd never been more hurt, exhausted, or anxious.

The last was his fault. Since the first moment she'd seen him he'd made her as nervous as a drunkard in a minefield.

"'Tis cold," Ruadri said as he stopped just behind her. His scent rolled over her. He smelled of something darkly decadent and spicy, like a chocolate spiked with serrano. "You should come inside, out of the wind."

Come inside with you, and find a dark room, and throw myself at you, yes. Oh, please, yes. The chill seeping through the wool cloak Emeline wore was suddenly biting, or was it his worry, growing sharper? *He doesnae care about me. I'm just a great bausy nuisance.*

"I'm no' a bairn."

"Aye, that I ken," Ruadri said as he came to stand beside her. He held out his huge black and amber plaid tartan. "You're shivering. Wrap yourself in this."

He was too close now, and any moment he would touch her with those large, strong hands that looked so capable and clever. Emeline didn't think she could stand that, and then the sensory wall inside her head begin to crumble.

"No, thank you."

Blast her ankle, she had to get away from him this instant. Emeline limped away, stopping at the edge of the river to pull back her hood and look down at the blurry reflection of herself in the ice, made only more vivid by the sunrise. For weeks she'd been a battered, starved prisoner, and it showed. So many snarls tangled her black hair it resembled a mass of poorly-done dreadlocks. The yellowish-brown bruises on the puffy side of her face made it look like a moldy cheese wheel. Her mouth seemed like a smear of faded red paint beneath the sunken hollows of her eyes.

Death oan a pirn stick, her grandmother would have said. Emeline had to admit she did look deathly sick.

A shadow stretched over her reflection like the wings of some fallen angel. "If you keep walking in that splint you may shatter that ankle, Healer."

Before she could stop herself, Emeline turned to face the shaman's broad chest. Well over two meters tall, and as wide as two caber tossers, Ruadri completely dwarfed her. She wondered if she simply talked to that wall of muscle that this time she might maintain her composure. But no, she couldn't see the shaman and not look up into his striking face, or his enigmatic gray eyes, the color of moon shadows. Silver spilled from his temples into his hair in two wide swaths, chasing the blue-violet glints that dawn had painted on some of the black strands.

Handsome men made Emeline nervous. Ruadri stunned and terrified her.

"I'm no' cold. My ankle's mending. I've told you I'll look after myself." She realized her voice had risen almost to a shout, and quickly dragged in a steadying breath. "I've been through an ordeal, Shaman. All I wish is to be left alone."

"I cannae do that," Ruadri said. "Ever."

He sounded so grim that it should have frightened her. The shaman's stature and bulk begged the inevitable comparison to the biblical Goliath, but when he moved he seemed more feline than giant. He also made no noise when he did. Everything about him radiated calm and quiet, except his eyes. He looked at her as if she were the only person in the world.

It reminded Emeline of how she'd felt the moment she'd first seen him, soundlessly approaching her in this very same spot, and her hands curled into fists.

He doesn't want you. He's an immortal, like

Cadeyrn. You're weak and worthless. No one wants you.

"Why willnae you leave me alone?"

"Visitors arenae permitted to leave the stronghold without an escort," Ruadri told her, as if she were asking a genuine question. "'Tis the chieftain's orders."

Of course, it was. The man wouldn't be chasing her unless commanded to.

"What does Brennus imagine I'll do? Run away, with a broken ankle?"

Without waiting for an answer, she hobbled around him and headed back to the rockfall spilling down one side of the plateau. The shaman followed her to the cluster of weathered stone tors that formed Dun Mor's labyrinthian front gate. Like the other rescued women Emeline had been shown how to navigate through its narrow channels. Still, every time she banged a shoulder or knee on one of the stone columns it infuriated her. Why did the Skaraven insist on keeping these ridiculous safeguards when they were out in the middle of nowhere? Hadn't the door been invented yet?

The end of her cane slipped on an icy

patch of stone, and Emeline pitched forward, throwing out her hands to break her fall. A brawny arm sashed her waist from behind and clamped her back against the shaman, who with a single motion swung her up against his massive chest.

Emeline would have told him to put her down, but wordless torrents of emotions cascaded into her own seething temper. Physical contact with another person now plugged her directly into their emotions. She floundered in Ruadri's feelings as they whirled through her. A honeyed flood of melting amber desire spread out beneath mists of dark blue frustration, stroking and clutching at her simultaneously. Sparkling tangerine enchantment spangled an endlessly flowering wall of green frustration. Holding her made his golden need expand to engulf the negative emotions, but not before something bubbled up inside her. Murky mists filled a corner in her head, but black instead of dark blue like his, and hers kept growing and spreading.

"Please put me down," she begged him.

When he did she staggered backward into the stronghold, nearly collapsing again.

Breaking the physical contact ended most of the empathic connection, but remnants of Ruadri's cognizance still pulsed inside her, softer now as they sifted into her own feelings.

He's so strong and kind and fetching. I cannae have him. I'll never have anyone.

And there was the true reason she hated the bridal shop in Inverness: because she'd never be loved. No man would ever want to marry her.

Once he saw she was steady Ruadri nodded and retreated to the chamber where he practiced his dubious healing arts. With him he took his emotions, finally releasing her from the connection.

The relief Emeline expected didn't come. Instead she was even more wretched. Was she mad to want to follow him, and reach out to him, and beg him to help her? Or was it the blackness growing inside her? Something had changed her, eating away at her normally placid temper and making her lash out. It roiled in her heart, restless and hungry, and made her do things she'd never have done.

Every hour she spent at Dun Mor it grew worse.

Standing there at the front of the clan's great hall, Emeline felt the weight of watching eyes, and took in the dozens of immortal medieval warriors gathered to work there. Dressed in basic, primitive tunics and trousers that didn't quite fit their big, heavily-muscled frames, the Scotsmen looked like a small army of stone lifters from some ancient highland games day. All of them possessed an alertness about them, as if prepared at any moment to engage an enemy on the battlefield. Yet they gave close attention to their tasks as well. The clansmen honed blades and spears, cut belts and purses out of leather, and even mended tears and rents in garments with bone needles and thick thread wound on sticks. Some were watching her, as palace guards did tourists, but most only spared her a glance before returning to their tasks.

Their collective curiosity curled and thrummed around her like a huge, purring tabby.

Emeline could block the feelings of a large group easier than those from a single person, so she reinforced her emotional walls. She might be nothing to look at, but she was a woman. Until Althea had married Brennus and joined the clan, the Skaraven had never had any contact with females. The shaman carrying her in probably hadn't set well with the clansmen, either. In this era men did not put hands on any woman unless he was marrying or burying her.

She felt an urge to go and find Althea and the Thomas sisters, but what would be the point? They didn't care about her, not really.

I've no friends here.

That thought made her miss Meribeth even more. They'd both worked at Fleming's Hospital since they'd graduated nursing school, and they'd had such a lovely friendship. That had been thanks to Meri, who charmed everyone she met, made everything fun, and had insisted on including Emeline in everything she did. Since her parents had passed away she'd been like a rowboat set adrift, so she'd felt privileged to have such a friend. How dismal and lonely her life would have been without Meri.

In the future her best friend had gotten married without her, and by now had returned from her honeymoon in France to set up her new house. Meri's wealthy neurosurgeon husband had also convinced her to quit nursing, so she wouldn't be at Fleming's. She had no idea that crazy time-traveling druids had stolen Emeline from Inverness just after she'd left the bridal shop. Meri would be immersed in her wonderful marriage. She certainly wouldn't spare a thought for a best friend who couldn't be bothered to show up for her wedding.

Jealous of their closeness, Lauren would have encouraged that. Emeline could even hear her nasal voice tearing her to pieces: *After all you've done for that stupid cow, Meri, she disappears on the most important day of your life. If she'd done that to me I'd never speak to her again.*

None of the Skaraven would speak to her, either. How self-satisfied they were in their masculine perfection. Emeline wished she had been born male, so she could pick a fight with one of the great haughty beasts and skelp him senseless. The grand, glorious Skaraven might be the finest warriors of all time, but they were still men. She knew exactly where to stick a dagger to slice through the–

What are you thinking?

She couldn't kill any of the Skaraven. No one could. They had all been made immortal. They were also good, decent men. Their war master, Cadeyrn, had risked his life countless times to rescue her and the other women. She'd be dead if he had left her behind, which he never had.

But he'd thought about it. That was why he looked at me so often during the escape. Even if I didnae feel it, I saw it in those cold eyes. Each time deciding if I was worth all the trouble…

"Emeline."

The slender, copper-haired woman who called her name rushed to her, followed by the dark, imposing figure of her husband, Chieftain Brennus Skaraven.

"You look so pale. Haven't you been able to sleep?" Althea Jarden knew better than to touch her, but looked all over her, her worry plain in her aquamarine eyes. "Did you hurt yourself again?"

I never hurt myself, Emeline wanted to shriek. *Those demented druids and their brutes did this to me. So did the other women and the Skaraven and every damned person around me since I left that huddy bridal shop. I've done naught but help others the whole of my life and still all of you DID THIS TO ME.*

"I'm well enough."

It took every scrap of her self-control to get those three words out. She swallowed all the hateful things she really wanted to scream in the botanist's face. How much longer could she keep holding them back? She could also feel the wet warmth on her wounded side, which meant the gash from the spear had begun bleeding again.

Althea shivered and wrapped her arms around her waist. "You should try and get some rest."

In that moment Emeline really saw how effortlessly beautiful the other woman was. No wonder Brennus had fallen so hard for her. Compared to Emeline she looked like a goddess.

Meribeth had never pitied Emeline like this, although now their friendship seemed very odd. The other nurse had been obsessed with keeping her own body very trim, almost to the point of gauntness. Why would she want to be seen with a walking lardy cake?

Of course, Emeline thought, swaying a little.

If you want to look a skelf, befriend a bulfie lass like me.

They should never have been friends. Meri had worked in surgery, while Emeline had been firmly entrenched in geriatrics. A sleek, fashionable girl from the city didn't take up with a girl from a village so small they had yet to pave the roads. All Meri liked to do on her off days was shop, have her hair and nails done, and throw parties or go clubbing. Taught by her parents to live their ideal of a quiet life, Emeline read books, knitted and gardened.

They'd had absolutely nothing in common.

Meri had always dragged her out of her flat to accompany her on countless adventures. Which when she thought about it had been Meri mostly having the fun while Emeline watched or waited or held her purse. No one ever spoke directly to her whenever Meri could be chatted up instead. Whenever she went out with her best friend Emeline listened and smiled and quietly seethed, just as she had in the dress shop.

As she did now with Althea.

"Emmie?" The botanist looked worried. "Are you sure you're all right?"

No longer trusting herself to speak, Emeline nodded, and then shifted her gaze to Althea's husband. The chieftain's dark eyes and austere features betrayed none of his feelings, but she could sense his emotions as clearly as if he'd flung a handful of thorns in her face. He considered her a nuisance, and wanted her gone from Dun Mor.

You may get your wish sooner than you think, you snaiking skellum.

Taking a tighter grip on her cane, Emeline walked past him and limped downstairs to her room.

Chapter Two

INSIDE HIS HEALING chamber Ruadri sorted the scant bundles the clan's gatherers had brought to him from their daily delves through the *Am Monadh Ruadh*. Only when a sharp, bitter scent filled his head did he realize he'd instead mangled them. Murmuring an entreaty to the Gods under his breath didn't soothe him, nor did tidying up the mess he'd made of the last of the Red Hills' autumn herbs.

"Now I turn a daft gowk." He brushed bits of the crushed greenery from his palms, wishing he could do the same with his troubles.

Bracing his big hands on the edge of the table, Ruadri bowed his head and focused on the pitted stone surface. He'd carved the slabs of the table himself, chiseling the granite out of a slope and carrying them back to the stronghold balanced on one shoulder. He'd been mortal at the time, and yet still the toughest of the clan. Now that he had risen from his grave, an immortal warrior who would never again age or know sickness or disease, he was as helpless as a swaddled bairn.

For that he could blame nothing but his inability to resist the intoxicating allure of Emeline McAra.

Ruadri had first seen the healer from the future just before he'd been awakened to immortality. He'd been pushed out of a void of blackness onto a narrow lane of strange stone. He'd known at once that he'd stepped into the future from the unfamiliar surroundings. Towering buildings of perfect brick penned him in the lane, and huge boxy carts of metal and fine glass had sped past him on fat black wheels. One silver cart with a red circle and the Roman letters I and T painted in white within it stopped beside him and blasted a hooting sound. A door in the brick building opened, and Emeline had hurried out.

"Take me to Bridge Street," she said to the man inside the cart.

Her voice sounded ragged, and Ruadri saw the tears shimmering in her bright eyes. Without thinking he reached out to her, and then the ground shook under his boots. The pebbly stone of the road cracked and collapsed as one of the *famhairean* emerged from the earth. It had been bespelled to look more human, but he recognized the way it moved, like some jerking, disjointed poppet. With one hand it caught hold of the silver cart, wrenching a side panel open and dragging out the terrified lady.

"Dinnae touch her," Ruadri shouted.

He'd drawn his dagger and lunged at the giant, only to pass through it as if he were no more substantial than a twilight mist. It had felt as if his heart would shrivel to nothing to discover himself a wraith, until he'd finally realized he was only having a dream of this, and her. The *famhair* pushed the helpless lass into the rent in the street, and then she was gone, and with her the whole of her world.

The next thing Ruadri recalled was fighting his way out of the earth, bursting forth from the cold, hard soil with the rest of the Skaraven. From the moment he'd learned that five females had been brought back in time by the mad druids and their *famhairean*, he had hoped to find the dark lady of his vision. Indeed, he dreamed of her every night. In the end it had been Cadeyrn, the clan's war master, who had found and rescued Emeline and the other lasses, and brought them to Dun Mor.

That, too, had been a bitter draught for Ruadri's pride to swallow.

Still, he would never forget the first moment he'd seen Emeline. Gods, but the lovely dream of her from his visions paled beside the real lady. She had skin as pale and perfect as white heather petals, and eyes so clear and blue they seemed pieces of sky. Her pretty mouth reminded him of the curves of blush-colored rose petals beginning to bloom. It had stabbed at him to look at her beautiful face and see the bruises that yet mottled one side of it. Water-traveling with Cadeyrn had soaked her ragged garments, molding them to her glorious body. Such luscious curves would have made a fertility goddess seethe with envy.

While her beauty made Ruadri's longing for her flare into rampant desire, the warmth of her spirit enveloped him in something he'd been unable to name. The heat of the hearth, the softness of goose down, the rush of cool water—she had something of all and yet none of them. What the healer made him feel he'd never experienced, even those long past nights when he'd lain shackled beneath a pleasure lass.

Ruadri understood the call of male to female, but he'd never felt it until now. Was this what other men endured when they met their intended mates? All he could think clearly on was his wanting, to go to Emeline McAra, and carry her off to his chamber, and claim her as his…but she would have none of him.

And why should she?

Unlike the rest of the Skaraven Clan, Ruadri had been sired and trained in secret by a tree-knower. Since boyhood he'd also been compelled to spy on his brothers and report back to the druids. Although he had finally been released from his onerous furtive duties, he would always be a half-blood and a traitor.

Naught can make me clean again.

"Shaman."

He looked up blindly as a tall, dark figure entered the chamber, and belatedly straightened. *Brennus should ken what I've done. Only then shall it be over.* But revealing the truth of his blood, and his long betrayal of the clan, would part him from Emeline, and that he couldn't bear just yet.

"How may I serve, Chieftain?"

"You carried the McAra healer into the stronghold," Brennus reminded him. "Explain to me why."

"I but caught her when she slipped in the tors." He briefly described what had happened, and then added, "To prevent another spill I reckoned I should. She's stubborn."

Dark eyes studied his face. "Aye, but she's made it plain that she doesnae crave your help, lad."

So, everyone in the stronghold knew of her dislike of him. Ruadri shrugged away the hurt of that acknowledged fact.

"'Twas naught but instinct. Another time, I'll let her tumble."

"And I'll invite the *famhairean* for a feast with the clan." Brennus arched a black brow. "I ken you had visions of the lass, Brother. I had the same of Althea before the tree-knowers awakened us. 'Tis hard to resist the urge to protect the lady. But the healer's blood-kin of the McAra."

"You'll no' give her to the laird," Ruadri said flatly. "Maddock hasnae claim on a female in truth no' yet born. She—" He stopped himself from betraying more than his concern over more than her wounds. "Forgive me, Chieftain, I dinnae mean to challenge you."

"Good. The last time you did, you near broke my facking sword arm." The chieftain's expression tightened. "That lass has something more brewing in her kettle, and I've the notion it'll soon spill out. My gut tells me 'twill be naught good. Do you ken what so vexes her?"

So Brennus had also noticed Emeline's uneven temper. "I cannae tell you certain, but I reckon 'twas what she endured at the hands of the *famhairean*. She's a gentle lady, accustomed to far better. What harms the spirit cannae be easily healed or forgotten."

The chieftain's gaze narrowed. "Aye, your words have weight. Cade tells me that the McAra healer has a mind gift. She keenly feels what others do."

"Likely 'tis the cause, then." Ruadri kept his expression blank, but the revelation was a fist to his gut. Emeline knew what he felt for her? Gods above, but he had never once guarded his emotions in her presence. "I should look at the wounds of the other lasses if they're rested. I managed but bandaging last night."

"Althea's gone to look in on them." He rubbed a hand over the back of his neck. "A wife and four more females under my care now. Oft I'd rather face a Roman legion on the march. 'Tis easier to battle a brute than fathom a female." Shaking his head, he left the chamber.

That the chieftain was so perplexed by the lasses' presence didn't trouble Ruadri. Like all the Skaraven, Brennus would fight to the death to protect them. Learning that Emeline was an empath, however, made clear the reason for her immediate rejection and dislike of him. Each time he'd been near her he'd felt longing and admiration and even possessiveness. Since they'd never met outside of his vision she wouldn't have understood his emotions.

No wonder she'd refused to let him touch her. If she'd sensed his feelings for her the lass probably thought him deranged with lust.

Ruadri grabbed what herbs and bandages he needed for wound care and left his chamber, telling one of the men in the hall that he would return shortly. From there he descended to Dun Mor's lower levels and went directly to the chamber Brennus had given to Emeline. He lifted his hand to knock, and then heard a whimper of pain. He pushed the door open and hurried inside, stopping short as he saw Emeline perched on the bed.

She'd stripped to the waist, and had only a shaped band of blue lace covering her breasts. Dark bruises and old wounds covered her torso from shoulders to hips, and she'd been starved enough to make her rib bones show. An open bottle of whiskey, cut threads, a pair of shears and scarlet-strained bandages lay beside her. More blood seeped from a partly-stitched gash in her side. Her trembling hand held a needle with thin thread connected to the wound.

He stared at the gash, which appeared much deeper and serious than she had led him to believe. Remembering to shove back his alarm, he asked, "Lass, what do you now?"

"I'm replacing some sutures." Carefully she tied off the thread before she snipped it. "A few broke when I slipped. What do you want this time?"

The ire in her glance told him she wanted him gone, but Ruadri could no more leave her like this than he could have let her fall.

"Brennus told me of your gift," he said, marching over to the bed to stand over her. "I came to say that you've the wrong notion of me, my lady."

"Have I?" Emeline looked down at the needle in her bloodied fingers. "I'm sorry for that."

She sounded indifferent, which likely meant she didn't believe him. He could work on her opinion of him later. For now, he needed to tend to her.

"I ken how to stitch shut a gash, and you cannae see all the wound. Permit me do this work."

"Such eagerness to put hands on me." Her eyes took on a peculiar narrowness as she met his gaze. "That's truly why you came. To be alone with me, where no one can interfere."

Her suspicions dumbfounded him for a moment. *Interfere in what?*

"'Tis but my way to look in on the wounded. If you dinnae wish it done here, we'll return to my healing chamber," Ruadri offered. "I shall send for Althea, or Lily, to be with you."

Emeline peered up at him. "Do you reckon you're the first to want to have at me? Lads in my time always wondered if I'd be good in bed. Fat lasses such as me, dinnae you ken, ever so desperate for it."

"Fat?" he echoed blankly. "What?"

"Baggie, chuffie, girthie." She threw out the words as if spitting them. "A great hauchan, one nurse called me. I ken what I look like, Shaman. I've endured this podgy body all of my life."

Ruadri peered at her. Even half-starved Emeline was the most luscious, beautiful female he'd ever seen, and she spoke of herself as if she were utterly blind.

"Have you hit your head as well?"

"Dinnae joke." She rose to her feet, swaying a little. "'Tis why you willnae leave me be. Because like all men you reckon I should be begging for it. When I've done naught but tell you to stay away. You should be made to listen."

That she believed he wished to force himself on her sickened him, but the thought of others attempting the same enraged him. What manner of men had she known in her time?

"You're mistaken," Ruadri said and saw how the dark of her eyes had dwindled to pinpricks, and glanced down. She'd clenched her fist around the shears she still held, as if she meant to drive them into his gut. "Emeline, no."

The door behind him opened, and a

willowy, blonde-haired woman carrying a bucket of steaming water came in.

"Morning, Shaman," Lily Stover said as she breezed past him. "This is blistering hot, Em, so be careful." The British woman set down the bucket and looked from the healer to Ruadri, wariness darkening her green eyes. "Am I interrupting?"

He watched Emeline's eyes change to how they had been before her outburst, and her hand slowly lowered the shears. If she had been drugged she could not have shaken off the effects so quickly. He could not sense any magic at work, either. Yet if he pressed the issue she might descend into that furious state again and attack them both.

"No, my lady." It took all his resolve to regard Lily as if nothing had happened. "I'll leave you to it."

Ruadri went from Emeline's chamber to the great hall, where Brennus and his wife stood with Rowan and Perrin Thomas. For a moment he struggled with what he should tell his chieftain and the other ladies. Something was terribly wrong with Emeline, and it wasn't simply lingering emotional trauma from the terrible abuse she'd endured. Althea had told him the nurse was the sweetest, gentlest woman she'd ever known, and Cadeyrn had spoken at length on her courage and ingenuity.

A lady's character did not change that much overnight. But what more had been done to her to alter her so? Had Hendry and Murdina somehow bespelled her, and then masked the magic to prevent detection?

Being half-druid and having some skill in the magical arts did not make Ruadri an expert on the tree-knowers or their powers. His sadistic father had hidden much from him during his boyhood training, doubtless to keep the upper hand. Emeline was not only McAra blood-kin but a druidess with a remarkable gift. Before he could help her, he had to discover what could possibly afflict her so, and if it required a treatment particular to her kind.

"There you are." Althea smiled as he joined them. "Everything all right?"

"'Twill be, my lady," Ruadri assured her. "Do you ken where Master Flen may be now?"

"Probably on his way to the McAra's stronghold for our meeting," the chieftain's wife said. "Why?"

৩৶৩

AFTER LEAVING the Thomas sisters to wait for Ruadri in the shaman's healing chamber Althea went over to the hearth in the great hall, where Lily stood speaking with Brennus and Cadeyrn. Their conversation halted as soon as they saw her, and the chief looked worried, which meant the topic wasn't a happy one.

"You can tell me what the problem is now," she warned them in a low voice, "or I can beat it out of my husband later."

Cadeyrn and Brennus exchanged an amused look, but Lily's grim expression didn't change.

"We've got a problem, all right," the British woman said. She hesitated before she added, "I think Emeline's about to go barmy on us."

Chapter Three

❧

DARK WATERS BROKE as Hendry Greum came up from the depths, his eyes momentarily dazzled by the glints of sunlight on the loch's rippling surface. The forest surrounding the ruins of the Wood Dream's ancient settlement remained as still and empty as the waters, thanks to a ritual that had been interrupted over a thousand years past. Despite the passage of time he could still remember the day his tribe had been wiped out by the Romans. It seemed a fitting tribute to the massacred druids that in all that time not a single living thing had come to dwell in this place. Hendry imagined that one day the entire world would be very much the same.

The only difference was the magic, of course. Once he and his *famhairean* killed off the last of mortal and druid kind, the realm would be reborn, and the age of his *caraidean* would begin.

"Everything shall be healed," he murmured, but his words made the air seem to shiver in response.

It mattered little to Hendry. Swimming in the loch where he'd long ago intended to drown himself pleased him. How brief and useless his life might have been had he clung to the path ever walked by druid kind. Instead he had turned his back on death to seize a forbidden fruit offered so sweetly to him. He'd never regretted his mating with Murdina Stroud, or the price they had paid for their love. Nor did he mourn the thousand years they had spent trapped in stone for their supposed wrongdoings.

Made immortal by the very druids who had imprisoned them, Hendry and Murdina would never die now—as neither would the *famhairean*.

A chilly mist wafted around Hendry as he waded to the rocky bank, where a much larger, broader *famhair* waited with his bathing robe. To see Ochd now gratified him, for he'd spent a great deal of time and magic reworking the giant's wooden body to closely resemble that of mortal kind.

For everything to work according to their plan, Ochd had to seem human.

"Fair morning," Hendry said as he took the dry linen and shrugged into it. "My thanks for your concern, but you shouldnae stray so close to the bank."

The only weakness the *famhairean* possessed was their reaction to water, which Hendry had gone to great lengths to keep secret. Any contact made the giants begin to revert to their natural tree forms. Full immersion trapped their immortal spirits in their submerged bodies, rendering them incapable of escape. He'd always considered it tragic that the druids had chosen to imprison the *famhairean* in a bespelled wood henge. They might have fared better with imprisonment by sinking the giants to the bottom of a loch.

The *famhair's* new, luminous eyes searched the horizon. "Aon says the cottage shall be finished by nightfall. Do we track the Skaraven tomorrow?"

The normal grating sound of the giants' speech had almost disappeared from Ochd's voice. With a little more refinement and practice, the *famhair* would be able to deceive anyone he spoke to.

"Tomorrow, Hendry?" the giant repeated.

"They use water to travel, and we cannae," Hendry reminded him, and gestured for Ochd to accompany him as he walked up into the forest. "Next we must fashion new bodies for the *caraidean* we lost in battle with the Skaraven." He saw how the giant bunched his fists. "Rowan shall come to no harm among the clan."

Ochd stopped to stare down at him. His newly-refined features had become capable of expressions, and his appeared bleak. "'Tis no' her place to be with them."

"Aye, and when 'tis time we shall take her back," Hendry assured the giant. A flutter of red caught his eye. "Return to camp now and help the others with the rebuilding."

Instead of obeying, the giant clamped a

big hand on the druid's shoulder. "Rowan isnae theirs. She belong to us."

"*Belongs* to us," Hendry absently corrected. "Go along now and help your brethren. I must tend to my dearest one."

Ochd glanced over at the figure flitting around the trunk of a dead elm tree. "So must I."

"And you shall, my friend."

Hendry chuckled and patted the *famhair* on his bulging hard arm before he went to intercept his mate.

Murdina vanished before he could reach her, but he knew this game, and stretched out beneath the leafless branches to wait.

"I followed you again, Hendry Greum," she called to him, her voice higher and softer than usual. "I ken what you do here. I watch you from the forest."

"I but wait for you, sweeting mine." He closed his eyes and heard her creep closer. "You must be quiet. You dinnae wish to bring your mother or father."

"They say I must marry that jobby Dirkus. He stinks of cow shite." She planted her feet on either side of his legs and lowered herself onto his lap. "I like how you smell, Hendry. Like the forest on fire. Fire…"

Knowing that she was remembering nearly being burned to death at the mill, Hendry pulled her against him. Rubbing his cheek against her nearly-bald head, he stroked her spine with a soothing palm.

"'Tis no fire here, only us. The cottage shall be finished tonight, and we will sleep in our own bed."

Murdina sat up and frowned at him. "I dinnae sleep with you. Mother ties me to the cot in her room." She giggled. "Only she doesnae knot the cord so well."

The fire had tampered with her already fractured mind, sending Murdina back to the age of sixteen, the time she likely considered the safest. Now she capered and played in the forest like the wild thing she'd been as a young lass, unaware that centuries had passed. She no longer recalled being bespelled and trapped in the Storr on Skye, or how it had slowly driven her mad. Hendry was almost grateful for her regression, as it spared her so much pain. He only wondered how long her delusions would last before she reverted to the broken, fearful woman she had become.

"Would you wish to share my bed, sweeting mine?" Hendry asked, caressing her cheek.

She pursed her lips, as adorably as she had when she'd been but a young mortal lass. "Shall we but sleep together? Or do you mean to take my maidenhood?"

"I shall want both." He drew her lips down to his, and kissed her tenderly, feeling the dark hunger rising in them together, as it always had.

Murdina drew back, frowning as she studied him. "You've so much silver in your hair." Her lips trembled as she stared at the back of her own hand. "And I've spots on my flesh, and wrinkles." She rose and skittered away from him. "How did this happen?"

"'Tis naught but illusion, beloved mine." Quickly he murmured under his breath and released his power to envelope her. The spell he cast transformed her appearance into that of the girl she had been twelve centuries past, complete to the soft fawn robe she had most loved to wear. As he stood he cast a second spell over his own body so that she would see him young again as well. "Forgive me. I meant only to amuse you."

"Oh, Hendry." Sobbing now, she hurled herself into his arms. "I never wish to be an old hag. I couldnae bear it."

"Then I shall keep you young forever," he promised.

❧

OCHD MADE his way through the deserted Wood Dream settlement to where Aon and the others labored on resurrecting Hendry and Murdina's dwelling. To fill the spaces between the timbers supporting the roof beams, the *famhairean* had stacked squares of turf atop a base of flat stones. More wood had been fitted over the lifeless soil to form a floor.

But nothing could fill the hollow that had grown inside Ochd since Rowan had escaped.

The rebuilt cottage's shoddy construction would not last, but it needed only to please Murdina. Since the mill fire she had lost her grip on time and reality, and instead dwelled in her dreams. Ochd secretly envied her, for he sometimes longed for the simplicity of the life he'd possessed among the Wood Dream. Standing as guardian and watching the tribe had filled his days with purpose and peace.

All the more reason to have Rowan back. The dark druidess never made him feel so empty or useless.

"Ochd." Aon, the leader of the giants, came to stand beside him and surveyed the work. "You find trace of Coig?"

He shook his head. "No' on the wind or in the trees. He didnae return with the others unbodied by the Skaraven."

"Coig couldnae die," Aon said, his voice flinty. "Mayhap they hold him."

"Naught could trap Coig," Dha said.

The largest of the giants, he pushed between them as he carried armfuls of thatching over to the cottage. When another *famhair* collided with him, he lashed out, sending the smaller giant and bundles of straw flying into the trees.

Ochd knew how angry all the *famhairean* had been since their latest battle with the Skaraven, but for once he didn't share their fury. He suspected that since their awakening

Coig had been slowly going mad. Time and again he had ignored orders to torment and torture the druidesses they had taken from the future. He'd been particularly cruel to Lily, the gilded-haired mind-mover who had—with a captured Skaraven—engineered the escape of all the females. Before the battle Ochd had worried that Coig might even harm Hendry and Murdina to feed his sadistic pleasures.

"I dinnae care for how Hendry changes you," Aon said, looking all over him. "Too human."

Before Hendry had taken Rowan and the other females Ochd would have agreed. Like the rest of his brethren even the thought of mortal kind had always enraged and disgusted him. Too long they had carried the memories of the Roman massacre. Knowing the dark druidess from the future, however, had drawn Ochd back to a past he'd almost forgotten. Rowan had changed him more than Hendry's magic.

"'Tis for our time to come," he told Aon. "What we shall do, 'tis more important than what 'twas done to us and the tribe."

Aon took in his scent, nodded slowly, and

went to stop Dha from unbodying the hapless *famhair* he'd tossed aside.

Ochd knew the druids would be occupied with each other for some time, just as his sullen brethren would continue their work until they finished the cottage. He walked toward the immense pile of thatching as if to collect more for the roof, and then slipped away into the trees. After the McAra Clan had become the Skaraven's mortal allies, they had provided each of the warriors with fine mounts. When Hendry and Murdina had escaped from the mill farm, the McAra laird and his men had pursued, cornered and nearly captured them. From what the druids said it had something to do with an ancient debt the McAra had owed to the Skaraven for more than a thousand years.

They yet did not know where the Skaraven hid from them, but the McAra might. The laird and one of the druidesses from the future shared the same name.

Descending into the earth as quietly as he could, Ochd burrowed deep. At the point where his passage would not leave a furrow in the surface, he tunneled away from the settlement. Like all *famhairean* he could move through soil at unstoppable speeds and navigate his way by reading the roots that crossed his path. It took him hardly any time to cross the many leagues to the midlands where he emerged from the depths.

From the edge of the wide glen he could see Laird Maddock McAra's men on horseback patrolling the outer perimeter of the stronghold's lands. Moving back into the shadows of a snowy evergreen patch, he watched and calculated their circuits as he sampled the unseen volatiles in the air.

Rowan had not been brought to the McAra's castle—Ochd would have smelled her in the wind—and that disappointed him. The Skaraven must still be keeping the druidesses at their hidden stronghold. He felt the tightness inside that he experienced whenever he thought of her among others unfriendly to the *famhairean*. She had no place being with the Pritani killers.

Rowan belonged to him, and he would find her and bring her back to safety.

Shaking off the soil that still clung to him,

Ochd crossed the open land between the last and next patrols, and dug under the high wall that surrounded McAra's stronghold. Following the roots of an old alder, he surfaced just behind the wide trunk. The towering tree, though some yards from the castle, had a thick branch that nearly touched the stones of the second floor. He quickly scaled the trunk and edged out along the limb, careful to remain among the thick leaves. Silently parting the foliage, he could see into one of the narrow windows.

The small laird stood inside speaking with a manservant while his female and some of their younger bairns sat on the floor engaged with some painted sticks and a small ball of string. For a long moment the sight fascinated Ochd, who had never seen a group of mortals do anything but run from him in terror. McAra's wife laughed as her children batted the string ball to bounce against Maddock's boot. The laird bent down and caught the ball to toss it back, grinning as well. The Wood Dream tribe had been much the same, Ochd recalled, in showing much affection to their bairns.

This was what Hendry meant when he spoke of family.

"…when they all arrive on the morrow," the laird was saying. "Prepare the largest chambers in the guest quarters for Chieftain Brennus and his lady wife. The old druid shall have the warmest room near the kitchen garden. Double the household guards as well, Steward. 'Tis some bad blood between the Skaraven and Flen."

"If the parley doesnae go well, my lord," the steward said, frowning, "should the men be told to separate the chieftain and the druid?"

The McAra shook his head. "If it comes to that, lad, I'll step in."

The remainder of the conversation proved unbeneficial, but Ochd lingered to soak up the sunlight and restore his power. It gave him the chance to watch the mortals until the laird and his wife led their bairns out of the solar. He then reluctantly left as he had come, and traveled back to the settlement, taking care to shake off every trace of soil before rejoining the others at the rebuilt cottage.

Aon beckoned to him. "Where you go?"

"I needed sun," Ochd said, and released enough of the power he'd absorbed at the McAra stronghold to make his changed flesh briefly shimmer. "'Tis good work you do here. It shall make Murdina happy again."

The other giant scowled. "Cottage willnae fix her."

Ochd wanted to tell his leader that nothing could do that, but held his tongue. Out of deference to Hendry they had all skirted her madness by indulging her crazed wishes. Soon Murdina would lose her mind altogether, and that might very well drive her lover to madness as well.

At that moment the druids came out of the forest. Both looked so young that Ochd almost didn't recognize them. He knew he should tell Hendry that he had gone to the McAra stronghold. The meeting between Brennus Skaraven and Bhaltair Flen would likely involve new strategies to be taken against the lovers and the *famhairean*. Hendry would no doubt wish to attack and kill the chieftain and the druid. But that would not serve Ochd's purposes. He could not follow Brennus through water, but he could question the old druid.

"My love, look," Murdina squealed.

She rushed to the cottage, laughing as she hugged Tri, who lifted her and spun her around.

"Well done," Hendry said, smiling as he went to join her.

Ochd said nothing but simply watched instead. This is how it would be when he took back his lady.

Chapter Four

WHEN RUADRI RETURNED to his healing chamber he found Althea and the Thomas sisters waiting for him. Last night they had assured him they had no grievous wounds. They'd both shown such exhaustion that after bandaging the younger sister's injured shoulder he'd agreed to wait and properly tend to them this morning.

In the light of his chamber, he could see their striking differences. Rowan, the darker sister, had a sturdy build, skilled-looking hands, and vivid features. Unlike the other lasses her skin still held the rosy bloom of good health, attesting to her depth of endurance. Althea had said that in their time

Rowan had worked as a carpenter, and throughout their ordeal had remained the strongest and most defiant of the ladies. The tight set of her jaw and narrowness of her eyes suggested she was presently hiding some source of pain, likely from the deep spear gash in her shoulder.

Hiding what she felt, Ruadri sensed, was not one of Rowan's talents.

By comparison the fairer sister, Perrin, appeared gaunt and weak. He saw the cause at once in her pale, dry skin, sunken eyes and emaciated limbs. Her delicate features seemed pinched, but not with pain. She had been a dancer, according to Brennus's lady, though now she looked hardly hale enough to walk. But he was reassured that her eyes remained clear and her dull gold hair had not yet begun to fall out. With proper rest and ample food, she would likely recover from the bodily effects.

The harm to Perrin's spirit from being starved might take longer to heal.

What puzzled Ruadri was how the two ladies could be sisters. They were nothing alike. He knew siblings sometimes shared no common physical characteristics, but there seemed a strong divergence of personality as well. Perrin remained silent and appeared nervous, almost tremulous, while her sister scowled directly at him as if prepared to attack.

"I don't need some medieval quack shoving moldy leaves and sheep shit into my wound," she told him before anyone could speak. "So if that's your plan, forget it."

"I use fresh herbs, my lady, and never, ah, dung." He studied the way she was standing and suspected her pain to be even greater than he'd guessed. "Mayhap you'll permit me to begin by examining your shoulder."

"Look at my sister first." Rowan nodded at Perrin, who cringed as Ruadri regarded her. "She took a hit to the back of her head, and the lump is still the size of a golf ball."

He glanced at Althea. "Golf?"

"A ball used in a game, about this size." With her fingers she measured a small circle in the air. "You guys won't invent it for another hundred years or so."

He nodded and approached Perrin. "Would you lift your hair from the spot, my lady?" Once she did he could see the rounded swelling, just atop the inion, where the bottom of her skull attached to the neck muscle. "Does it yet hurt you?"

"I've had a headache since it happened," the dancer admitted, glancing at her sister.

"Tell him the rest," Rowan said.

Perrin sighed. "It's wrecked my druid thing. Since the mad druids brought us here I've had visions almost every day. After Lily knocked me out they stopped completely."

"If I may touch your head?" Ruadri waited for her nod, and then carefully felt around the swelling for fractures. But Perrin showed no sign of discomfort. "Have you felt confused, unbalanced, or stomach-sick?"

"Not at all." The dancer rubbed her temple. "The headache isn't that bad. Actually, it seems to be going away now."

Ruadri came around and brought a candle close to her face, noting how her eyes responded as they should to the nearness of the light.

"Setting her on fire isn't going to help," Rowan said, taking a step closer.

"Relax, Fight Club," Althea told her

before he could reply. "He needs to check her pupils, and they don't have penlights in this century."

The dark lass made a rude sound. "I thought you weren't a medical doctor."

"See how I'm letting her have the last word?" the botanist asked Ruadri. "I think I've grown."

"No signs of bleeding from within. I feel naught broken." He set the candle aside. "I'll make a poultice for the swelling, my lady. If you've any changes for the worse you should come to me at once. I reckon with rest and food you should feel better in a few days."

"Okay." The tension went out of her shoulders. "What about my visions? Will they ever come back?"

No injury could remove the power bestowed on her by passing through the sacred grove's time portal. To tell her that would reveal too much of his knowledge of druid kind, however.

"Mayhap, once you've healed."

"Which means he doesn't know," Rowan put in.

"Why would he?" her sister countered.

"Not like he's a druid or went to medical school."

Guilt made Ruadri turn away. He busied himself by taking a small linen pouch and filling it with herbs to make a compress, using lavender, mint and sage along with some dried heather flowers for her headache.

"Soak this in warm water before you apply it to the swelling, Mistress Thomas," he said to Perrin, and then regarded Althea. "She needs food and rest as much. If you would, my lady, ask Kelturan to prepare his bone brew and a bolstering pottage for her."

Brennus's wife tucked her arm through the dancer's. "Come on and I'll show you the kitchens. You're going to love our clan cook. Well, not really, but as the chieftain's lady I'm not supposed to refer to him as the annoying medieval blockhead he is." She glanced at Rowan. "Don't worry. I'll guard her with my life. Which is immortal now, so…"

"Fine," the dark lass said with a snarl. When the two ladies left she turned her ire on him. "I've got more than a bump on the head going on here, and you're not an MD. Where's Emeline?"

"In her chambers." The shaman recalled how Lily's presence had seemed to calm the nurse and wondered if Rowan would do the same for her. "I'll send for her, if you wish."

Relief flickered through her dark eyes. "Yeah, that would be awesome."

He summoned a sentry, who returned a short time later with Emeline. The nurse had changed into clean garments, and looked annoyed but otherwise clear-headed as she hobbled into his healing chamber.

"Hey, Flor– Ah, Emmie," Rowan quickly corrected herself. "Would you mind looking at my shoulder? Nothing against Witchdoctor Mountain here, but I'd rather have someone from the twenty-first century patch me up."

"On the table, please." She didn't spare Ruadri a glance. "I'll need shears."

"Permit me." Drawing his sharpest dagger, he carefully slit the sleeve and yoke of Rowan's tunic.

Emeline lifted the edge of the linen he'd tied over her injury last night. "It looks infected, and the bandage has stuck to the wound. We'll want to soak it."

He brought her a bowl of meltwater he'd

earlier boiled and let cool, and she poured a small amount onto the bandage. Rowan's jaw tightened, but she remained silent as Emeline slowly peeled away the sodden cloth. The deep graze and the flesh around it appeared reddened and swollen, and Ruadri saw the seep of festering around something still lodged in the center.

"'Twas done with a spear?" he asked Rowan, who nodded. "A piece broke off when it struck you, mayhap."

"Of course, it did." The dark lass looked up at Emeline. "How are you at minor surgery, McAra?"

"My hands arenae as steady as I'd like." Now her blue eyes shifted to Ruadri. "Wash your blade with whiskey, dry it with a clean cloth, and then run it through the candle flame. Once it's sterile I'll tell you how to cut."

"Wonderful." Rowan closed her eyes.

Ruadri knew how to clean a wound knife properly but held his tongue as he followed Emeline's instructions. Once he had prepared the blade, he fetched some cloth to place under her shoulder for the drainage.

"She'll first want a draught for the pain,"

he murmured to the nurse.

"No need. Rowan laughs at pain, dinnae you, lass?" Emeline said, her voice taking on a harsh edge.

"Yeah, sure." The carpenter frowned. "Just get it over with, Shaman."

"Cut here." The nurse made a short gesture over the swelling to indicate the place and length.

Ruadri applied the blade, opening the wound and releasing a stream of bloody fluid. Rowan hissed in a breath, and at her sides her hands fisted. She yelped as something caught on the edge of the knife.

He leaned down to peer at the spot. "'Tis a shard of wood, lodged in the center. I cannae tell how deeply."

"Cut around it," Emeline said. When he stared at her, she made an impatient sound and tried to take the blade from him. "My hands have steadied. Give it to me."

"I've got a great idea," their patient said, looking alarmed now. "Why don't *I* pull it out?"

The nurse's expression darkened. "You dinnae ken anything about healing."

"But I've got wood mojo, remember?" Rowan lifted her hand to the wound.

Ruadri caught Emeline's wrist when she tried to grab the dark lass's hand, and pulled her away from the table. "Mayhap you should wait outside, my lady."

With her free hand she slapped him, and while the blow only stung his cheek the unexpected attack put him on his heels. A heartbeat later Emeline shoved him aside and lunged at Rowan.

"Hey." The carpenter rolled off the table, backing into a rack of drying herbs. "Take it easy, I got it." She held up a long, bloody splinter.

Emeline uttered a low, furious sound as she came around the table.

"I said to leave it to me, you stupit wench."

"Okay, Florence, calm down," Rowan cautioned her and glanced at Ruadri as he came up behind Emeline. "It's all good now."

The nurse's cane whistled in the air as she tried to hit Rowan over the head. "I told you no' to call me that."

The dark lass dodged the blow and shoved the drying rack over between her and the nurse. Her eyes widened as Emeline picked up the rack and tossed it aside.

"Emmie, come on. I was just joking. You know I'm your friend. Or I try to be. Sometimes."

"Friend." The nurse's expression twisted as she pushed Rowan against the wall, and then plucked Ruadri's blade from the table. "You're naught but fresh meat to carve."

The chieftain's half-brother came into the chamber holding a delicate chain in one of his scarred hands. "Ru, I've managed this much for you–" He stopped in his tracks just as Ruadri grabbed the nurse from behind and Rowan snatched the dagger from her. "By the Gods." He rushed over to help.

Emeline screamed and struggled wildly as she fought to free herself from Ruadri's grip. As he turned to move her away from the dark lass she seized a stone pestle and hurled it at Kanyth. The heavy bowl bounced off the weapons master's skull, and he fell to his knees before toppling onto his side.

"I'll put you all back in the dirt," Emeline said, her voice so low and rough now she sounded like one of the *famhairean*. "'Tis where your kind belong, feeding the worms. *Let go of me.*"

Ruadri kept an arm clamped around her waist as he reached for one of his vials. Removing the cork with his teeth, he lifted and put the nurse on his work table. There he kept her pinned as he brought the potion bottle to her lips and poured a measure of its contents into her mouth.

Emeline spat it back in his face. "I'll tear off your head, human, slow–"

She choked as he poured another measure into her mouth, and then pinched her nose shut to force her to swallow.

"I got this guy," Rowan said as she went to kneel beside Kanyth. "He looks a lot like Brennus. Great. She had to knock out the chieftain's bro. Don't hurt her, Shaman."

"Never would I." Ruadri looked down into Emeline's eyes, which became dazed as her eyelashes fluttered. "Dinnae fight it, lass. 'Twill no' hurt you. Only rest now."

It took another minute before his sleeping potion took effect. Tears slid down her flushed cheeks when at last she closed her eyes and went limp.

"Okay, Hammer Time, up we go," the dark lass said as she helped a groaning Kanyth to his feet. "Shaman, you got any more of those head compresses?"

Ruadri kept his arm across Emeline's waist as he glanced over at the weapons master, who swatted at the blood streaking down one side of his face. "He needs but a swim in the river to heal."

"Why would the lady attack me?" Kanyth demanded. "I've done naught." He glanced at the necklace he still held and then at Ruadri. "It couldnae be this could it?"

"This isn't about you—or you," Rowan told Ruadri. "When we stepped out of line Hendry and Murdina's guards used to knock us around and beat us with sticks, the same way Emmie was fighting just now. They were too strong to use their fists. And you heard what she said, right?"

Ruadri nodded. "Why would she call us humans, and wish to kill us?"

"She wouldn't." The dark lass eyed the unconscious nurse. "But that's exactly how those *famhairean* assholes talk."

Chapter Five

GATHERING IN THE great hall
and gabbing incessantly seemed to
be the Skaraven's only way to deal
with crises, not that Rowan really cared. Her
newly-stitched   shoulder   throbbed   like
someone was steadily whacking it with a club.
She had the same light-headed buzz she used
to get in her time just after donating blood.
With so many huge men around, she had to
constantly squelch the urge to run for the
nearest exit. All the fight had been shocked the
hell out of her. She was operating in flight
mode now.

But neither bothered her as much as why
Emeline had attacked her.

Rowan actually liked the Scottish nurse,

who she considered to be the only genuinely nice woman in the bunch. Since being brought back to Never-Ending Medieval Fest, Emeline had worked herself into exhaustion trying to take care of everyone. She'd never let any of them go off the deep end. She'd made rounds like the nurse she was in order to check on them and talk to them. Sometimes she'd even joked about the lack of food, water, and creature comforts that had made them so miserable.

Emeline had also never laid a hand in anger on anyone except Rowan just after they'd arrived at the stronghold. But that had been just a girly slap she'd definitely earned. Thing was, Emeline didn't slap or punch or hurt anyone, ever. No matter how bad it had gotten, she'd always tried to help—until today.

Listening to Althea tell Brennus all about it while Ruadri listened was pissing off Rowan, too. The botanist hadn't even been in the room.

"She's been under tremendous stress since they took us," Althea told her husband, though not with much conviction. "Maybe she finally snapped."

"I don't think so," Rowan said and pushed herself off the edge of the table where she'd perched. "Emeline doesn't snap. Not in the barn, the cage, the granary, and definitely not any time while we were on the run. She nagged or she puked or she bitched, and a few times she cried, but she never once lost it. Ask Lily, who, by the way, didn't open her mouth once during the first week of Fun at the Forest Farm."

Everyone glanced over at the chef, who spread her hands. "In my defense, I'd just had my neck broken and then healed by time travel. Also, the voice took a spot longer to come back."

"It's not a criticism. I'm just saying." Rowan regarded the shaman, who hadn't uttered a peep since Brennus's guards had carried Emeline to the underground levels. "You're the medieval medic. Something is seriously off with Emmie. Did the crazy couple do something to her, or can't you tell?"

"I couldnae sense any lingering spell work," Ruadri said, his cavernous voice sounding almost angry. "I searched her garments for charms but found none. From what I ken of the lady, whatever compelled her wasnae by choice."

Rowan would have mentioned that the shaman had known Emeline for all of two minutes, but that wouldn't help the cause. "There you go," she told the chieftain. "Maybe the guards did something to her. She was talking and acting like them when she went postal on me."

"More the reason to keep the lass apart from others," Brennus said.

No wonder he'd fallen in love with Althea. They were both thick as a brick.

"But she's our friend, and she's in trouble," Rowan reminded him. "This is not the time to go all chieftain on her. She needs some help here."

"All we ken is that the lady near skewered you, and felled my weapons master," Brennus said. "I and my lady shall be some days at the McAra stronghold. Until we return, Lady Emeline shall be kept in the *eagalsloc*. From there she can hurt no one, nor come to harm."

"The eagle's what?" Rowan demanded. "I don't speak Gaelic."

Althea grimaced. "It's the clan's…confinement area. I stayed there myself for a bit." She cleared her throat. "She'll be perfectly safe, I promise."

"I must see to preparations for our journey, my ladies." Brennus's dark eyes shifted to the shaman. "Once we reach the McAra's I shall consult with Bhaltair Flen on the matter. Until we ken the cause of Lady Emeline's affliction, she remains below. Keep watch over her, Ru." He nodded to Rowan and Lily before he strode off toward the stables.

The shaman stared after him before he went in the opposite direction.

Oh, this was *so* not happening on her watch, Rowan thought, and turned to the idiot redhead.

"Say, Doc, you haven't given me the whole underground castle tour yet, and I'm just dying to see the place." She looped her arm through Althea's and clamped it to her side. "Excuse us, Lil." Rowan nodded at the men. "Guys."

"The only thing back here is my brother-in-law's forge," Althea said as Rowan hustled her into the nearest empty corridor. "Also,

Kanyth likes me and is conscious now, so if you start hitting me he'll probably–"

"I'm not going to punch you, you idiot." As soon as they were out of earshot of the men in the great hall Rowan dragged her to a halt. "What are you doing, going along with this? They locked up Emmie. *Emmie.* She's a *nurse*, for God's sake. And what the hell is this *eagalsloc* thing anyway?"

"You're not going to like it," the botanist warned her. When Rowan fisted her hand and took a step closer she heaved a sigh. "Fine. It's an oubliette."

Rowan pinched the bridge of her nose to keep from punching Althea. "Just FYI, I don't speak French, either."

"It's a deep pit in the ground accessible only by a rope ladder lowered from the edge. Which Brennus has no doubt removed." Quickly she raised her hands in a gesture of surrender. "Try to see it from his point of view. Emeline didn't just knock out his half-brother. Kanyth is a clanmaster, second only to the chieftain in rank. And she *was* trying to kill you, Rowan. No one goes that crazy and still gets to wander around the stronghold."

She stared at Althea in disbelief. "You really have no idea what you've done. That woman kept the rest of us alive. She did it with a bashed face and a broken ankle. She couldn't even eat for days after the last time Coig—oh, but I forgot. You weren't in the cage with us starving and freezing and waiting for the next beating. You were here playing flip the kilt with Brennus."

The other woman's light blue eyes glittered. "You're right. I wasn't there for whatever they did to you after I escaped. I was too busy trying to convince the Skaraven to help us. And, if you recall, I came back with the clan to rescue your ass, which also killed me. Brennus selfishly took a little time to bring my frozen body back here to bury me. He and the clan were lowering me into a grave when the immortality thing kicked in. Lucky for you I did reboot." She leaned close. "Or you might still be starving in a cage."

"You're breaking my heart, Doc," Rowan snarled back at her. "Cade and Lily got us out, not you. You killed yourself trying to save the Scotsman and his crew. Whatever. Nothing makes it okay to toss Emeline in a freaking prison pit. Give her to me, and I'll take her to the portal and send her back to our—" She stopped as she saw something flicker over Althea's face. "What?"

"In the state she's in, Emeline can't go back to the future. She could do worse to the people there than she did to you today." The botanist backed away a few steps. "She can't stay at Dun Mor, either."

Rowan folded her arms. "I know Brennus is pissed about his brother, but come on. You can't kick her out in the snow for it."

"It's not that. We've learned that Emeline is likely a direct descendent of our mortal allies, the McAra Clan. She and the laird, Maddock McAra, look so much alike they could be siblings." When Rowan rolled her hand, she added, "Women in this time have very few rights, and the rules about unmarried females are very strict. Custom demands that because she's blood-kin she should be handed over to Maddock."

"Handed over?" Rowan's jaw dropped. "For what?"

"For whatever he wants to do with her. He's the laird," Althea said slowly. "We won't do that, of course. But if McAra discovers we brought Emeline here without telling him anything about her… It's basically considered the same as holding her hostage. It's the kind of thing that could start a war between the clans, Rowan."

One of the guards entered the hall and stopped a short distance away. "Forgive me, my lady, but you're needed. Lady Lily finds the kitchens in want of some changes…" He winced as the bonging sound of an iron pot hitting the floor came from behind him. "… that arenae amenable to Kelturan."

"Well, nothing is." Althea regarded Rowan. "Look, while we're at the McAra stronghold we'll talk to the druid and see if he knows how to help Emeline. I promise you, whatever Brennus decides, I won't let anyone hurt her." She hurried off with the guard.

Rowan considered banging her head against the wall, but it was made of solid stone and she'd probably crack her aching skull open. Even if she could talk her way past the sentries posted on the lower levels, with her messed-up shoulder she couldn't haul Emeline out of the pit. Especially not if the nurse still wanted to kill her. That was the part that really hurt, worse than the shoulder.

I thought she liked me.

For once Rowan's perpetual urge to go and check on Perrin didn't kick in. Whatever brainwashing their adopted mother Marion had done to make her watch over her sister for eternity, it seemed to have worn off or faded away. As soon as she learned of it, Perrin had made it very clear that she didn't want a bodyguard anymore. Rowan should have been relieved, even happy. Protecting her sister, however, had occupied—had defined—nearly her whole life. Without that responsibility she was lost and alone, and then it struck her. Althea had Brennus, and Lily had Cadeyrn. The clan would protect Perrin now, and Emeline had been dropped in an inescapable pit.

No one needs me anymore.

Rowan wandered down the hall toward the forge, but then felt a waft of cold air and followed it down another passage with an odd, swinging stone door. Pushing through it, she found herself outside the stronghold and in another maze of piled stone. Boot prints in the snow led her through that and into a stone tunnel that widened and opened into what looked like a gigantic primitive barn. Every part of the stable looked clean and tidy. Even the dirt floor had been well-oiled and packed down. Not a single Skaraven occupied the place, which made Rowan wonder who looked after the animals. Whoever he was, the clan should give him a raise. He kept the place spotless.

The newly-built wooden stalls stretched out in four long rows, and when she stepped inside a dozen horses' heads appeared over the pegged doors. She walked over to the first onlooker, a huge white stallion with gleaming dark bronze eyes. Making sure he could see her straight on, she checked his ears, which stood up and pointed at her—aka happy horse ears.

"Hey, big fella." She didn't know if he was a biter, so she couldn't pet him. Keeping her voice low and soft, she asked, "You're okay with me barging in here?"

The stallion nickered back what Rowan took as a yes. For some reason that simple response made her eyes burn.

At least the damn horse likes me.

She walked past the stalls to the ladder that led to a second-level storage loft and glanced up. Tidy bales of hay occupied most of the space, but she saw the edge of a dark wool blanket tucked in the middle of the stacks. Climbing up the ladder, she glanced over her shoulder before she stepped onto the deck and inspected the makeshift bed. Whoever had been sleeping up here had covered a pile of hay with the blanket and folded the corners to make a crude mattress. She envied him. Since coming to this time she'd slept in far worse places.

The hard, sharp voice of her internal foreman immediately gave notice: *Pull it together, Thomas.*

Carefully she lowered herself onto the blanket and stretched out on her uninjured side. She didn't mind the smell of hay and horses, or the fainter scent the last occupant had left on the wool. Whoever slept in the stables smelled like leather and pine, with a dash of sweat. She'd forgotten how much she liked Eau de Working Man. Maybe she'd wait around for him and see what sort of highlander he was. Probably some oversized, muscle-bound, ready-to-rumble type like the rest of the clan. God, she was so tired.

You're not going to cry.

Closing her eyes, Rowan finally let the tears brimming on her lashes spill. She never wept around anyone else, not since the first time Marion had punished her as a girl. The old hag had enjoyed making her break down, so she'd learned to swallow the sobs and shut down the waterworks. Even now she did it silently, holding herself with her good arm and pressing her face into the blanket.

Congratulations. You've turned into a girl.

Weeping thankfully led to sleeping. In the dense darkness Rowan still felt lost, but at least no nightmares came. She'd barely closed her eyes since being yanked back through time, and she was so done with the fourteenth century. Done with the cold and pain and terror. Sick of being disliked by, well, basically everyone on both sides. Finished with always being the resilient one, the one expected to defend, to take the beating, to refuse to cower. Rowan knew she didn't play well with others, and she'd never suck up for the sake of acceptance, but she had tried to protect Perrin and the other women.

When would someone be there for her? Strong for her? Devoted to her?

A dream came, stroking warmth along her cheek, and Rowan turned toward it. She smelled the man again, more leather than pine this time, and felt a new ache in the bottom of her belly. Such a tender touch from such a hard hand seemed impossible, but it feathered over her skin like drifting down. She could feel it mapping her face, from the arch of her brow to the curve of her chin. His thumb swept the remnant tears from her cheeks, and his fingertips tidied the mess of hair framing her temples.

No one in her life had ever touched her so reverently.

Although she knew it would end the lovely sensation, Rowan opened her eyes, and saw that she hadn't been dreaming. A lean man in a shabby tunic and leather trousers crouched beside her. A mane of shining, white-blonde hair surrounded his unsmiling face, shadowing its angles and lines. His hair was so pale it should have made him look old, but it didn't.

It had been cut recently, judging by the uneven ends.

She should have sat up, said something, or knocked his hand away, but she couldn't stop staring into his vivid eyes. What color were they? Caribbean blue, with a dash of emerald, or maybe dark turquoise inlaid with green garnet? Whatever shade they could be called, they were the most mesmerizing eyes on the planet.

He seemed just as fascinated by hers.

Rowan reached up, intending to push his hand from her face, and found herself pressing it against her cheek. Twinkling sensations popped out from under his palm and moved down her neck and into her chest, like a thousand unseen sparks trying to kindle something. Her heart? Had anything ever felt this exciting? Nothing, not even when she'd watched Perrin dance. She couldn't look away from his face, and when he closed his eyes for a moment she understood.

Too much, too fast, too soon.

She'd known this before, too, this wonderfully bizarre rightness. Yet she could not for the life of her remember when that had been.

Maybe she'd day-dreamed now and then about finding a man she could love, but her imagination couldn't bring a fantasy to life. Besides, she'd never once been attracted to fair-haired men. Something about them always exasperated her.

Maybe because on some level she knew they were supposed to look like this guy, and yet never did.

No, this was definitely wrong. Who had this insane reaction to a complete stranger she could never have met? It didn't matter. She wouldn't mind staying clueless for the rest of her life, as long as she could keep looking at him.

"You came. Came to me." His low, almost rough voice barely registered above a murmur, and he spoke as if he hadn't for a long time. "I didnae think you real."

"Yeah. Same here." Either he could read her mind, or everything in her head was true. Hoping it was the latter, Rowan went with the first thing that popped into her head. "Where have you been?"

"Waiting. Watching." He drew her upright, taking care not to jar her shoulder.

Even the way he touched her was familiar. This whole thing was outrageous, and enchanting. Like getting mugged and seeing fireworks at the same time. It made her want to laugh out loud and burst into tears. For an awful moment she thought she might do both. Crying over a man she'd never met was not on her to-do list.

"It doesn't– This isn't real." Even as the words came out of her mouth, she knew it was, and met his gaze again. "I'm not dreaming, am I? You're real."

"As real as you. Tell me your name." Dread tinged his voice, as if she might give the wrong answer.

She swallowed against the vise of fear that had suddenly clamped around her throat. "Rowan Thomas."

His expression didn't change, but his gorgeous, glorious eyes filled with pleasure. "I am Taran Skaraven."

Chapter Six

❦

STANDING INSIDE THE rounded walls of the clan's aviary, Ruadri bound a tiny scroll to the bird in his hand. He had coded the message to Bhaltair Flen about Emeline and her affliction, in the event the McAra's dovecote master opened it. No mortal could read the cipher they used, but since all druid kind communicated in code he was sure it would arouse no suspicion. He could not wait another day or more for Brennus to consult with Bhaltair. The delay might cost the lady the last of her sanity.

If being cast in the *eagalsloc* hadn't already done so.

Releasing the messenger bird outside, Ruadri watched it fly off toward the midland

stronghold. He should return to his duties now
and look in on the Thomas sisters to assure
they improved. He told himself this very thing
even as he took a side entry and descended to
Dun Mor's subterranean levels. There he
crossed paths with Girom and Cenel, the two
clansmen assigned to sentry duty in the lower
levels. They were headed in the same
direction.

"Shaman," they said together, nodding
to him.

"What do you here?" Ruadri asked as he
collected the rope ladder and fastened it to the
edge hooks.

"Kelturan sent us," Girom told him,
nodding toward the dark interior of the pit.
He produced a cloth bundle. "We're to place
this near the edge. 'Tis to ward off the
Sluath."

Ruadri took the bundle and opened it to
see it had been stuffed with club moss and
yarrow. He vaguely remembered the old
Pritani superstition about storm-riding
demons who stole dying mortals and took
them to the underworld.

"'Tis nonsense."

"Aye," Girom said, taking back the bundle. He crouched and placed it by the pit. "But 'tis better than taking Kelturan's clout to my ear."

Cenel peered over the edge. "Should you go down alone, Shaman? 'Tis said that the lass dropped Kanyth with a single blow."

Ruadri just looked at him.

"Aye, right," Cenel said quickly. "You've no' Kanyth's soft head." The sentry nudged his partner. "Back to our posts, Gir."

Taking a torch from the wall bracket, Ruadri lowered the ladder and climbed down. His bulk made the rope creak, but as soon as he saw Emeline he dropped down onto his feet.

The guards had left her on a straw-stuffed fleece and covered her with his tartan. They'd also removed the broken splint from her ankle, likely on Brennus's orders. He would want her hobbled.

His anger faded as he planted the torch and simply looked his fill of her.

"I'm awake," she said, startling him, and opened her drowsy eyes. "I've been for some time. I heard the men talking."

Ruadri crouched down beside her. "Do

you mean the sentries? They looked in on you?"

Emeline nodded. "Girom finds me too pretty to be made an enemy of the clan. Cenel imagines I'd serve well as a fine pleasure lass, if I'd be the one chained to the bed." She met his gaze. "They really did chain you?"

"'Twas the custom." He would knock the men's heads together a few times for speaking so crassly within her hearing. "They shouldnae have said such."

"They thought me asleep." She glanced around them. "Why am I in a great hole?"

If Emeline couldn't recall attacking Rowan, then what plagued her might be affecting her mind.

"You've been afflicted, my lady. I dinnae ken how or by what yet, but 'twas none of your doing."

"But it was. I remember it. Feeling it." She pushed herself up into a sitting position, grimacing as she pressed a hand to her wounded side. "Something in me wanted to kill Rowan. Something dark and seething with hatred. If you hadnae…hadn't stopped me, I believe I would have."

She sounded like a different person now. Her Scottish accent had become lighter, and she had corrected herself to use the same words that the other lasses from the future spoke. Before now she had talked as if born in this time.

"Do you feel this presence now?" he asked.

Emeline started to shake her head, and then went still. "Aye—yes. It's still there, waiting. The first time I felt it I...." She ducked her head. "It started when I came out of the river, with the others. When I saw you, I was drawn to you. I also hated you. I told you not to touch me because I was afraid of what I might do."

If she had been somehow possessed by one of the *famhairean's* spirits, it could be fighting for control of her form. "'Tis speaking to you, trying to compel you, mayhap?"

"No. It's not a person. It doesn't have thoughts. Only feelings, but not like anything else. They're not natural." She took hold of his hand and, for a moment, he could only marvel at her soft touch. "I know it doesn't make sense, but I feel it the same way I feel you. Your worry over me. Your anger at the sentries. To me they're like a forest of snarled green knots, and a sky filled with hundreds of moons."

Ruadri had to blink and then yanked his hand free. "Forgive me, my lady. I didnae ken I'd harm you."

"You don't understand. You're not hurting me." She put her hand on his again. "Touching you helps me. It feels better."

As he stared at her small hand on his, something gnawed at the edges of his memory. Though he'd sworn never again to think on his training, something his sire had told him slowly came back

"Such talent," he finally said to Emeline. "'Tis a gift among druid kind. 'Tis called soul-sharing."

Understanding seemed to dawn on her face. "I think I might be one of them," she whispered. Though he thought she would continue, she stopped and looked at the floor. She took in a deep breath and brought her gaze up to his. "If you could feel something other than worried and angry, maybe it would make me stronger. Can you remember what you felt when you saw me by the river?"

Remember it? Those sentiments had near scored her name on his heart.

"Aye."

He cradled her hand between his as he remembered the deep, gratifying delight of seeing his lady on the riverbank. Of knowing at last that she was everything and more than what he had envisioned. Her beauty had rushed through him like a breeze in a garden of roses, and her voice had been the sweetest sound to grace his ears. He'd wanted so badly to embrace her that he'd lingered in the shadows, until he could better control that ravenous longing for her.

"Yes, that's what I felt." Emeline shifted closer, leaning into him. Her eyes became slumberous. "Like a river of flowing honey."

A strange, blissful warmth enveloped Ruadri, and he couldn't resist wrapping his arms around her. Holding her against him filled him with sensations he'd never before experienced. He could almost feel her unraveling the knots of his worry and dispelling the many moons of his anger. The heat expanded, sizzling along the curves of the skinwork on his arms, and yet it didn't alarm him as it should have.

Emeline tipped her head back, her breath quickening. "Oh, now I feel that."

"'Tis your touch. 'Tis how the soul-sharers best work their gift." For once he blessed his size and strength, for it would take all of it to release her. "What we do, 'tis dangerous, my lady."

"Oh, no, Ruadri." She slipped one hand around his neck, her fingers caressing his flesh. "Nothing that feels this good could hurt."

He felt her trembling despite her claim, and resolved to put her aside and move away. Yet his hands would have none of that when they could cup her lovely face, and feel the softness of her skin. They wanted every inch of her against him, under him, wrapped around him.

"You've enchanted me," he murmured, pressing his mouth to her brow before he looked into her eyes. "'Tis what you wish, my lady?"

She put her lips close to his ear. "I want everything, Shaman."

Ruadri felt the last of his reason crumble

as she turned her head and brushed her mouth over his. The petal-soft touch sent a surge of scalding desire through his veins, burning away all but the need for more. He had never kissed a woman, but the moment she parted her lips for him he had to taste her. She made a low, sweet sound as he licked the inner curve of her lip, and gripped his neck as she pressed against his chest.

If touching Emeline had been blissful, kissing her proved a delicious torment. He held her fast as he stroked her tongue with his, swallowing the moans and gasps she made. The scent of her rushed into his head, stoking his hunger to wild heights. Emeline's trembling fingers twined in his hair, and her breasts heaved until he could feel the pebbled peaks through their tunics. Her wanting fed his own, and his cock swelled hard and thick with throbbing need.

"Emeline." Saying her name parted their lips, and Ruadri drew back enough to see her expression. "'Tis better now?"

"I can't say." She whispered the words against his jaw. "I've never kissed a man."

"Nor I a lady." They should teach it,

Ruadri thought, for surely none had ever done so well with the thing as they had. "I speak of the affliction."

"What affliction?" she said against his mouth, slurring the words as she caressed him with her soft lips.

Ruadri forgot his intentions and shifted her into the cradle of his arm. He couldn't get enough of her sweetness, and the thrill of holding her made the pleasure so keen he thought he might never end the kiss. He knew he should, but she'd stolen away all of his will. Some days from now they'd be found locked together like this, and even then, it would take all the clan to pry them apart.

"Wait." She wrenched her mouth from his, and when he would have kissed her again she put her fingertips to his mouth. "Something's wrong. My ankle."

He heard her, but it took another moment to emerge from the sensual daze and put her at arm's length. "I hurt you?"

"No." She peered at her feet, and her eyes widened. "Look."

Ruadri turned his head and saw only a shapely foot with no bruising or swelling.

When he reached to touch it, a pale white glow radiated from his forearm to her flesh, settling in the cuts there and reshaping them into a crescent.

His moon had marked her, and it should have shocked him. Instead Ruadri traced the curving scar, feeling a possessive pride, and felt her shiver beneath the crescent.

"You've been healed," he told her, glancing at her flushed face. He saw no fear in her eyes, only bewilderment. "'Twas my battle spirit. It marked you with its crescent."

"But it didn't take away these feelings." Emeline pressed her hand to her abdomen. "I can still feel it growing, like an infection. But that's not right. I can't be sick. Cade told Lily that anyone with druid blood is healed of their wounds and illnesses after they come through a portal." Her shoulders drooped. "Maybe I'm not druid kind after all."

"If 'twere so, you wouldnae be such a powerful soul-sharer." Ruadri thought for a moment. "When you were with Hendry and Murdina at the mill, did either put hands on you?"

"They both did." A shudder ran through

her. "So did some of the *famhairean*. I always felt sick after it. Sometimes I couldn't hold down my food for the next day."

All became clear to Ruadri then. Over time she had likely absorbed through touch the druids' anger and lunacy, as well as the giants' blind hatred of all humans. Such a combination would have slowly driven any soul-sharer mad.

"'Tis how you became afflicted," he told her. "Emeline, you must dispel these dark feelings from you."

"I don't know how to do that. Do you?" When he shook his head, she wrapped her arms around her waist. "What happens now? Do I go crazy, like them?"

"No, my lady. I've sent a message to an old, wise druid who mayhap can help. I'll send another, urging his reply."

"We dinnae—don't have that much time." She swallowed hard. "It's growing too fast. I think in a few hours I'll lose control again, the way I did with Rowan. You should keep me here or toss me into a..." She paused and stared at him. "If you took me through a portal to a safe place, and then brought me back here, do you think it would remove the emotions they put inside me?"

Ruadri knew the sacred oak groves would heal damage done to any mortal with druid blood—both to the body and the spirit, according to what Galan had told him. To take her to the portal would defy Brennus's orders. He'd have to secret her out of the stronghold. Yet even if he returned her whole and well to Dun Mor, the chieftain might still choose to send her to her blood-kin. Then he realized how he could prevent that.

"We shall attempt it," he told her, and helped her to her feet. "Can you walk unhindered?"

Emeline took a few steps. "Yes. I'll need some boots, and a cloak to cover me." She smiled at him. "Thank you for this."

"'Twas your notion," he said, making himself smile back.

Ruadri guided her over to the rope ladder, and hoisted her up before he climbed with her out of the *eagalsloc*. Because she didn't know he was half-druid, she remained unaware that he could also control the portal. He would direct it to send her to the only place where she would be safe. There she would arrive healed and ready to go on living the life she'd been born to.

To keep Emeline from going mad, or becoming a pawn of the McAra, Ruadri had to send her to her own time.

Chapter Seven

CHILL AND WEARINESS took turns gnawing on Bhaltair Flen's bones as his mount clopped along the midlands road. Overhead flocks of small birds flitted hastily south, chased to warmer climes by the arrival of the bitter dark months of winter. He envied their wisdom, for if he'd had any sense he'd be safely installed in his cottage now, sipping brew by the hearth as he pondered matters important to no one but himself.

Only the cottage and his quiet life there had been destroyed. After finding the druid settlement abandoned, Hendry Greum and his *famhairean* had set fire to Bhaltair's home. According to reports from the druid watchers not even the old pear tree had survived the flames. It had been like losing part of himself. He'd lived in that cottage for all of his current incarnation, and two others before that. And while the loss of his home could not compare in scope to the many villages and countless lives destroyed by the mad druids and their giants, it was as if he'd lost yet another old friend.

Hendry had a talent for inflicting wounds that could never entirely heal.

Bhaltair knew some of his pain came from the exhaustion dogging him. He'd had no time to rest when he'd returned to Aviemore. The meeting with Brennus Skaraven and Maddock McAra demanded he set off for the midlands directly. The weight of his responsibilities challenged the limits of his strength and vitality, both of which he knew to be failing him. He'd been sleeping harder and deeper these last weeks, and had trouble rising near every morn.

Not for the first time did he wonder if he truly was getting too old to manage the onerous duties thrust upon him. What other druid of his age and stature trotted about the countryside chasing immortal warriors and their deranged enemies? Yet he would not complain, for it had been his grievous mistakes made in a previous life that had done much to help create this nightmare. It had been his plan to trap the immortal *famhairean* in a wood henge for all eternity. He'd also cast Hendry and Murdina into the stone of the Storr on Skye, also imprisoned there as immortals so they could not reincarnate.

It should have kept the mortal realm safe, but Bhaltair's plan had utterly failed. Something in the distant future had set all of them free, and they had returned to this time to take up again their evil work. Once they destroyed him and his tribe, the traitors meant to exterminate all human kind from the earth—and now they had the power to do so.

Bhaltair had summoned the only ally that druid kind had to stand against the mad druids and their giants: the Skaraven Clan. He had awakened them from their graves as immortals, and in return for the tremendous gift, he had asked they help protect mortal and druid kind. It had stunned him when they'd flatly refused and used their new powers to disappear into the highlands. Only recently had he been able to persuade Brennus Skaraven to meet and talk with him again on the matter.

This meeting at the McAra stronghold would be the most important of Bhaltair's existence. If he could not persuade the chieftain to fight once more for them, druid kind would be doomed to extinction. Ultimately, so would every living human in the world.

He left his troubled thoughts when his acolyte trotted up beside him. Oriana Embry's young face glowed with rosy color, and excitement sparkled in her usually serene eyes. "My thanks for permitting me to accompany you, Master. I shall attempt to make myself useful."

He gave her a reassuring smile. "You are that and a joy, my dear one."

Privately Bhaltair still wondered if he'd made the right decision in allowing her to join him on this sojourn. Oriana had barely begun her druid training with him, so she had few skills with which to defend herself. She'd also repeatedly shown contempt and anger toward the Skaraven Clan, whom she partly blamed for her grandfather Gwyn's gruesome death.

But the lass was very young and determined to be of use to him. Indeed, her devotion to serving and protecting Bhaltair had already caused her to defy his instructions several times and follow him into dangerous predicaments. This time he'd brought her along simply to keep her placated, and where he'd known she could come to no harm.

They reached the druid settlement at the edge of McAra territory late that afternoon. Along the edges of the midland pastures and grain fields stood a wide, dense stand of evergreens that seemed to stretch the length of the horizon. Several young druids in dark robes emerged from the tree cover. Carrying golden scythes, they moved to block the road.

"Name yourselves," one of the druids called out.

"Bhaltair Flen and Oriana Embry." He slowly dismounted and stood still as they approached for a closer inspection. "I sent word by dove to your headman to expect us."

"Forgive our caution, Master Flen," a red-haired youth said, coming forward and bowing low. "The havoc caused by the traitors and their monsters has made us all uneasy."

"Never apologize for protecting your tribe, lad," Bhaltair told him, and touched his shoulder. "I sent my own into hiding to do the same."

The other defenders took charge of the mounts, while Oriana unfastened their satchels and carried them into the trees. The pines and firs rustled around them before fading away as they breached the illusion spell, and entered a small, prosperous-looking settlement of cottages.

The Sky Thatch tribe had already harvested their food and spell gardens, and the surrounding fields had been well-readied for the cold season with layers of oak leaf and bog mud. Beneath the snow the layers would slowly rot and nourish the soil until the time came for spring planting. A bare-branched apple orchard behind some storage barns had also been properly prepared, the trunks of the youngest trees wrapped in protective hemp cloth to prevent the thin bark from frost-splitting.

The red-haired lad escorted them to the headman's cottage and waited until an even younger druid emerged before bowing and

departing. The headman's adolescent appearance belied his pure white hair and the
ancient craftiness in his eyes.

"I'd welcome you, old foe, but I dinnae
care for uttering falsehoods."

The insult made Bhaltair chuckle. "Nor
would I expect them from an elder with such
cheek as you, Fingal Tullach." He regarded
Oriana, who stared wide-eyed at the headman. "My acolyte, Oriana Embry, who now
thinks us both deranged."

"Mistress Embry." Fingal smiled and
bowed to her. "Come in and warm yourselves
by the hearth. Cora has used the last of her
strength to prepare hot brew and pottage
for you."

"I've more strength in my smallest finger
than you've in the whole of that skinny
carcass, Beloved," an older woman's voice
called from the cottage.

Inside the simply-furnished home a petite
elderly woman stood filling bowls on a table
with a thick vegetable stew. Her wrinkled face
and work-worn hands did not eclipse her
natural beauty, Bhaltair thought, but rendered
it more obvious, like a bloom shedding petals.

She glanced up and glared at Fingal before she regarded Bhaltair and Oriana with a more benign expression.

"Never listen to a word that comes from my husband's lips," Cora Tullach said, winking at Oriana. "He's ever the poor jester. I reckon the Gods must toss him from the well each time he arrives."

The young lass glanced at Fingal. "Forgive me, but the two of you are…mated?"

Both of the Tullachs laughed.

"Aye, lass, in this and every other incarnation," the headman told her. "We're destined to find each other no matter when we return from the well of stars—and to love no other."

Bhaltair was surprised to see Oriana's mouth flatten, and murmured to her, "They're soul-mated—pledged to share every incarnation as husband and wife."

"Ah." Her expression cleared. "I've heard of such, of course, but they're so rare."

"Aye, few like us will mate, for 'tis eternal, and the time of rebirth cannae be chosen. Likely when I next come back he'll be the old one, and we'll scandalize the next generation anew." Cora gazed fondly at Fingal. "We dinnae mind so much, even when we must wait for the other to grow enough to bond proper."

"'Tis a true testament to love and patience." Bhaltair saw his acolyte blink rapidly, as if fighting tears, and knew her sorrow over Gwyn's death remained keen. "Fingal, might I beg some joint salve, if you have any? My knee sorely plagues me."

"I've a crock in the back pantry," Cora told them as she picked up a covered basket. "I'm off now to look in on Magda and her new bairn." She nodded to Oriana before leaving the cottage.

Once he and the headman had moved out of the acolyte's earshot, Bhaltair said, "Some weeks past the lass lost her grandfather to torture and murder by the *famhairean*."

"Ah, that explains her forlorn looks." Fingal nodded as he stopped in front of a wall of shelves filled with pots, bottles and crockery. "With a troubled heart, she should be with her tribe."

"I cannae bring myself to send her home. She's an orphan with no blood-kin left, and they mean her for tending sheep." He grimaced. "She's a born speak-seer, Fin. Someday to become one of the most powerful among us, I believe."

"By the Gods. No wonder you keep her close." The headman took down a cloth-covered jar. "Cora makes this from heather flower, dock root and mallow leaf. I've more of the root, and yarrow as well, if you'd want a potion to help."

Bhaltair shook his head. "I've mead-owsweet for the pain. Dock root ever turns my teeth black and makes me doze, and my slumber has been too heavy of late. Fin, I shallnae take Oriana with me on the morrow. She's no' yet learned to guard her tongue, and I cannae risk riling the Skaraven. But if I leave her behind, she'll try to follow after me."

"Ever determined the young—as well I ken." The headman chuckled. "Leave her to us. We'll keep her from causing mischief. One of our brothers cares for injured birds, and among them he has a pair of newly-hatched owlets. I'll go to Magda's now and speak to Cora on arranging a visit in the morning."

Out at the dining table Oriana sat waiting

for him, her food untouched. "Do you wish me to help with your knee, Master?"

"'Twill wait." Bhaltair put down the salve crock before he eased down on the bench seat across from her. As soon as he smelled Cora's brew he knew it contained honey, which would likely keep him awake half the night. "I cannae drink sweet brew this so late," he told Oriana, pushing away the mug. "Would you fetch me a cup of water from the kitchen, dear one?"

"Of course, Master." The acolyte smiled as she rose and walked into the next room.

Bhaltair had little appetite, and noticed that the amount of pottage in Oriana's bowl was slightly less than his own. He switched the bowls, pouring half of his back into the pot to make it appear as if he'd eaten a portion.

"Mistress Tullach's broth smells delicious," Oriana said as she set down the cup beside him.

"'Tis the herbs she uses, I reckon." He forced down a few mouthfuls while he watched the lass devour her bowl. "I didnae remember to bring food for the journey here. Forgive me for starving you, dear one."

"You ate naught on the way either," she scolded gently, nodding at his unfinished bowl. "You should have the rest, to keep up your strength, Master."

With a sigh Bhaltair spooned up the last of the pottage, and then sipped some of the cool water she'd brought. "Oriana, when we're done here, I shall take you to visit your tribe."

"If 'tis your wish, Master, of course." She rested her chin on her hand. "I should like to show you my grandfather's home. He has...he had so many beautiful spell scrolls. He would spend every night illuminating them. I'd watch him at the work for hours."

He saw how her gaze had gone dreamy, as it often did when she retreated to happier times with her grandfather. Yet she was too young to have spent all her days doting on Gwyn. It perplexed him, for he knew his old friend preferred his solitude. Why hadn't Gwyn convinced Oriana to keep more company with druids of her own age?

"Perhaps 'twould be better to reunite with your friends among the tribe," Bhaltair suggested. "Surely they miss you as much."

"I had no friends. The other druidesses

didnae care for me." Her voice grew dull. "They spoke against me in secret, or when they reckoned I wouldnae hear. But I did. 'Twas very hard to bear. I oft thought…" A yawn interrupted her. "Gods above, but I'm so tired."

Filled with new sympathy, Bhaltair reached to pat her hand. "We all struggle with such dark feelings in the presence of one so naturally gifted as you."

Oriana blinked at him. "Did you envy Gwyn?"

"More oft than I care to recall." He sighed. "All who came to ken your grandfather loved him. He could charm anyone, but even more, he could truly befriend them. Never had I such sway over the hearts of others."

"No one loved him as I did." She rubbed her eyes before she slowly finished her pottage.

Past her shoulder he saw the bespelled night torches outside flare to life and shed their golden glow over Fingal and several older druids gathered around him. From their expressions they spoke of some amusement, for they laughed before parting. Seeing that small, simple exchange made him long for his own tribe, and talk of things that made them feel such happiness.

Tomorrow he would have none of that with Brennus Skaraven, but he would attempt to at least keep things civil. If the chieftain had wanted him dead, he would have killed him after the clan's awakening, at the old burial site. Bhaltair also suspected Brennus had not confided all to the McAra, or the laird would hardly welcome him.

I must make amends to the Skaraven for what was stolen from them, but how?

A thud brought his attention back to his acolyte, who had slumped over onto the table. Quickly he rose and went around to her, brushing back her hair to see the peaceful set of her face. The journey had tired her so much that she'd fallen asleep like a bairn, where she sat.

"Never worry, Oriana," he murmured to her. "When Fingal returns he shall carry you to bed, where you shall have naught but happy dreams."

Chapter Eight

E MELINE PULLED THE hood of the cloak down to shadow her face as Ruadri scanned the surrounding forest outside the stronghold. Although the darkness concealed them, the shaman had warned her that they still had to avoid the night patrols. Part of her didn't care, the part she now knew the mad druids and their giants had poisoned. To think that they'd contaminated her with their insane emotions still made her want to throw up. She'd never harmed another person in her life, but if this didn't work she'd become a murderous monster. Ruadri would have to put her back in the *eagalsloc*, where she'd spend what was left of her worthless life drowning in mindless hatred.

"I'm not worthless," Emeline muttered under her breath. "I'm a nurse. A healer. A good person."

A big hand folded over hers. "Stay with me, my lady."

"I will." She looked into the shaman's gray eyes as she drew on the steady warmth of his feelings. Just as when he had kissed her in the pit, his touch and emotions forced back some of the seething darkness. "Just don't let go of me."

As they made their way along an old trail Emeline expected to feel a twinge of pain from her ankle. That Ruadri's battle spirit had healed it seemed just as impossible as becoming infected with madly lethal emotions. Since being forced back through time Emeline had witnessed too many inexplicable things to doubt his claim. She also knew that Althea and Lily had been similarly marked after becoming close to their Skaraven lovers.

He's not my lover. He's a healer, and I'm his patient. That's why his battle spirit fixed my ankle. It's his job.

Ruadri stopped and drew her against his chest. "Dinnae make a sound or move," he told her as he lifted her off her feet with one arm and wrapped his tartan over her with the other.

Emeline rested her cheek against the broad expanse of his chest and closed her eyes. A faint sound of snow crunching came from the left of them, and then stopped.

"Shaman?"

"Aye, Manath, 'tis me," Ruadri answered, and splayed his hand over Emeline's spine, pressing her closer. "I'm for a walk to clear my head."

"So much beauty must muddle it," the sentry replied. "Does she fare better, your McAra?"

"In time she shall." Beneath the tartan his hand stroked from the center of her shoulder blades to the small of her back. "Fair night, Brother."

"And you, Shaman." More snow crunched as the clansman continued on his path.

Emeline let out the breath she'd been holding into Ruadri's tunic. Instead of releasing her, however Ruadri lowered her to the ground and kept rubbing her back with that slow, gentle sweep of his hand.

"I think he's gone," she whispered. "We should go now."

"Aye." Slowly he pulled away the folds of his tartan and took her hand in his. "But first I must assure no one follows."

He took out his dagger and cut a small branch from a nearby bush. With a touch as deft as a painter's, he smoothed out their tracks while leaving Manath's.

Ruadri glanced at the sky as snow began to drift down. "'Twill help cover our footprints."

As the shaman led her through the woods and down to the river, he lifted her off her feet again. Before Emeline could make a peep, he'd crossed the icy currents and put her down again on the opposite side. Once more he held onto her longer than was necessary, and she felt again his amber flood of desire, thicker and hotter now. He wanted to kiss her again, and if he did she would go crazy in a different way.

"Stop thinking about that," she said as she wriggled free. "Healing first. The rest we'll sort out when we return."

His emotions abruptly retreated. "Forgive me. 'Twas a memorable kiss."

"I'll never forget it." She tried to smile, but the dark anger roiled inside her. "We'd better hurry now."

Ruadri guided her through the brush until they reached the hidden portal. He boosted her up onto the rocks that formed a makeshift wall around it, and then lowered her down to the narrow ledge surrounding it.

"No, my lady," he said as she reached down to place her hand on the ground. "'Twill pull you in too quickly. Kneel beside me and brace your hands on either side of you."

Emeline didn't remember the mad druids having them do any of that to open the portal in her time. As she recalled, they'd simply thrown them on top of the ground, which then instantly vanished beneath them.

"You're certain about this?"

"The druids trained me in some of their ways." He watched her as she followed his instructions, and then propped one of his hands beside hers. "Clear your thoughts now, my lady."

She nodded, and saw the ground disappear as a twisting tunnel lined with oak branches opened only inches from her knees. "How do I tell the portal to take us to the forest farm?"

Ruadri leaned over and kissed her brow. "You dinnae need to."

Emeline saw him grab onto the rock behind him, and then he pushed her into the portal. Rage exploded inside her as she realized he was sending her through alone, and she flung her arm back, hooking it through his.

"Emeline, no."

The spinning vortex sucked them both inside. In her fury she jerked him closer, slamming their bodies together as they fell. She pummeled Ruadri with her fists, knowing she couldn't hurt him but determined to try. He'd been trying to hurt her, or kill her, she was sure of it. All human kind ever did was inflict pain and suffering on each other and every living thing. They deserved to be torn apart, as they had done to the Wood Dream.

When she purged the world of them…when she…

The rage inside her heart slowly evaporated, replaced by the opaque white light that radiated from the portal's walls to envelop them both. It was like every wonderful thing Emeline had ever touched, from the silky fine fur of a kitten to the thin, delicate cheek of a newborn bairn. She gasped as tendrils of yellow-streaked green smoke poured out of her eyes and mouth, vanishing as the light intensified.

All of the darkness inside her had gone, leaving only a hollow sensation.

The shaman cradled her face between his hands, and his regret washed over her like dusky lavender rain. His lips moved as he spoke, but she heard what he said only in her mind.

I but wished to save you from all harm, my lady.

Emeline no longer felt anything but Ruadri, and then they emerged into glaring daylight. He rolled with her so that he fell on his back, and she landed atop him. The sweet scent of wildflowers filled her lungs, and when she lifted her head she saw green everywhere around them. Fat bees buzzed from one bloom to the next. Different stones that appeared newly-carved surrounded them in a small, grassy clearing. The rocky slopes and ridges beyond the trees looked higher and much more rugged than the round-topped mountains around Dun Mor.

"Where are we?" she asked and glanced down at Ruadri, who was staring at the ring of stones.

"I cannae tell you." He sat up, which put her in the position of straddling his lap, though he seemed not to notice. "What did you think as we fell through the portal?"

"I knew what you'd done," she said, "and I wanted to hurt you." Gingerly she climbed off him and stood. The warm breeze on her cheek made her touch her face, which no longer felt bruised or swollen. Even the rat's nest of her hair now fell smooth and shiny over her shoulders. "Mostly the darkness wanted me to kill you, but that's gone now."

He rose and scanned the horizon. "I meant to protect you by sending you to your time."

"What if the portal hadn't healed me? I would have landed in my time as a crazy murderess." When he didn't reply she knelt down to reopen the portal. "I suppose it doesn't matter now that I'm all right. We need to go back before we're missed."

He stiffened and turned his head. With one hand he pulled her up and pushed her behind him as he faced the woods.

"Show yourselves," he demanded, in a tone so fierce she flinched.

Emeline peeked around his arm. "There's no one–"

She broke off with a gasp as she saw dozens of eyes blink open on the trees. The bark separated from the oaks, forming into a group of lean, rather short men who had painted their flesh to look like bark. Even their trousers had been dyed and embroidered to look like wood.

"Be you *dru-wid*?" the man at the very front demanded.

"You ken what we be, Pritani," Ruadri said in the same dialect, his voice rumbling like thunder from a sky-filling storm. "You watched us arrive."

Most of the men seemed more interested in her, Emeline noticed as she withstood their stares. The lead man muttered something, and he and the others removed the bark hoods covering their heads and stepped out into the sunlight. Each man wore his blue-black hair in thick queues loosely bound by thin braids woven with leafy vines. Their eyes turned crystalline blue in the sun, and their unpainted brows looked almost snowy white. All of them tossed fiery volleys of bright orange curiosity at her, a few tinged with small explosions of hot pink astonishment.

"They look just like me," she whispered to Ruadri. "Are they the McAra?"

"I think no' yet, lass." He glanced at the ground before he bowed and said to the lead man, "Ruadri mag Galan, shaman to the Skaraven tribe. Mishap brought me and my *bhean*, Emeline, here on our journey. We meant no trespass."

Why was he calling himself that odd name and referring to her as something even odder? Emeline knew better than to ask in front of the men, but it made her feel even more uneasy.

"The gods deliver you aside one who bears our image. 'Tis enough for welcome." The man returned his bow and extended his arm.

"Drest mag Ara. My ears dinnae ken the Skar-aven. Be you a highland tribe?"

"Aye," Ruadri answered.

Emeline breathed a sigh of relief as she watched the men clasp each other's forearms. She also noted that Ruadri matched the painted man's odd speech pattern. But at least it seemed there would be no violence, and the tribesman might be able to help them find their way back to Dun Mor.

"My sire awaits beyond the wood," Drest told them. "We've heard of how the Roman invaders plague your tribes of late. He shallnae give me peace if I dinnae offer *dru-wid* travelers a night of rest and food."

"The gods ever reward the generous." Ruadri bowed again. "Our thanks, Drest mag Ara."

Most of the men donned their camouflage and returned to their positions by the trees, but Drest and two others escorted Emeline and Ruadri from the glen. She wanted to ask a thousand questions, but feared she might say something to offend or even anger them. Ruadri held her hand loosely, but through the contact she could feel his determination to keep her safe, threaded with a glittering stream of sheer power. It rolled through her, ironing out her own worry and making her feel supremely safe, even in this situation.

Drest's village lay only a half-mile from the portal, and Emeline took care to memorize every landmark they passed. If they had to make a run for it, the portal offered their best chance to escape.

But why did it bring us here?

When they came out of the trees she saw a scattering of large round stone structures with high, cone-shaped thatched roofs. The big houses looked almost new, but their unsophisticated design reminded her of the old *brochs* around Scotland that dated back thousands of years. As the Pritani people came out of them, she also noticed how they wore very primitive garments made more of fur and hide than cloth. They didn't resemble the few natives she'd seen since arriving in the fourteenth century. The tribe looked as if they belonged more in the stone age.

An uneasy realization dawned, and Emeline tensed. But as she recalled the strange cadence of Drest's speech, something that had been in the back of her mind finally registered. When it had taken every ounce of will for her and the other women to survive the mad druids, no one had questioned the language.

How am I understanding their words? How have I understood anything?

She squeezed Ruadri's hand. "You said that they're not the McAra yet. What did you mean? And why did you call me a van?"

"'Twill keep, lass," he murmured back.

A lean, heavily-tattooed man with white feathers woven into his braids emerged from the largest *broch*. Two warriors armed with spears came to flank him as he walked toward Drest. The painted warrior bowed deeply before he turned to Ruadri and Emeline.

"Sire, these two tree-knowers sprang from the sacred circle on our watch," Drest said. "Shaman Ruadri mag Galan of the Skaraven tribe, and his *bhean*, Emeline." To them he said, "Our headman and my sire, Chieftain Ara Alba."

"'Tis an honor to greet you, Chieftain." Ruadri bowed over so far, he almost folded himself in half.

Ara nodded. "*Dru-wid* kind be ever welcome among us, ever now as the invaders march from the south. My *máthair* came from the Snow Fallen tribe." His gaze shifted to Emeline. "'Tis plain you share her bloodline, *Dru-widess*."

Emeline didn't know how to respond, and her cheeks heated as she bobbed in what she hoped was an appropriately deep, respectful curtsey.

Ara watched her for another long moment before he said, "Traveling be weary work. Drest, take the shaman and his *bhean* to the visitors' *broch*. Tonight, we shall share food and speak again."

Ruadri took Emeline's arm and draped it over his in an odd fashion, and walked with her as they followed the painted warrior to the other side of the village. The tribespeople didn't look directly at their faces as they passed, but she could feel their stares boring into her back. With every step she was more self-conscious, especially when she saw how some of the women pointed at her face and body. Two adolescent boys carrying deep bowls of steaming water and rough woven cloths met them at the entrance, and Drest directed them to place everything inside.

"We gather at sundown. I shall come for you," Ara's son told them, and then strode off in the direction of his father's house.

Ruadri ushered Emeline into the *broch*, and then pulled down a hide that had been pegged over the inside of the doorway. "Keep your voice low, lass," he advised her as he inspected the interior.

If Ara's tribe looked like they had just emerged from prehistory, the simple furnishings in the *broch* seemed to belong to cavemen. Everything from the crude table and shelf seating to stuffed furs mounded atop a bed platform fashioned of stacked stones made her feel uneasy. The stuffy, hot interior made sweat bead along her hairline until Ruadri took down the pieces of wood wedged in the narrow window openings, and a little breeze filtered in.

She went over to peer at a very skinny candle sticking out of a greasy rock. "This isn't a candle."

"'Tis a rush light," Ruadri said and came to join her. "They gather the old, great ones from the marsh, and peel away the husk. Once they soak the pith in fat and dry it, it burns well. Since rushes grow everywhere, the tribe neednae store them until winter comes."

"You talk as if you've done it." She watched him nod slowly, but she still couldn't quite believe it. "We're not in the fourteenth century anymore, are we?"

"No, lass." He gazed around them. "I spent my boyhood in a *broch* very much the same. They've no' been built in this fashion for a long time."

Her eyes burned with unshed ears, and she had to swallow several times before she could ask the only question she had left. "How long?"

"The portal brought us back to the beginning of your tribe, my lady. Ara Alba founded the McAra Clan." His jaw tightened as the rush light began to sputter out. "We've returned to the time of my mortal life: the first century."

Chapter Nine

SINCE COMING BACK to the old Wood Dream settlement, sleep for Murdina Stroud had become a nightly ordeal. Closing her eyes reminded her too much of being trapped in the darkness of the Storr. No crickets chirped, no owls screeched. Even the night wind seemed soundless. The terrible fire at the mill had left her so nervous that the crackle of the flames in the new hearth made her heart pound. Hendry sometimes made her a special brew that permitted her to rest without being tormented, but it no longer kept her asleep. The potion he secretly added to it had likely lost its potency, but she loved him for trying to help her rest.

He wishes only for me to feel at peace again. How can I tell him 'twill never happen?

Rolling onto her side, she watched firelight dance over her lover's face. By the Gods, but he looked so handsome. Since awakening as an immortal Hendry slept lightly, and if she touched him he would wake and pull her into his arms. Such a prospect tempted her. These new body wards that made them appear so young again had also stoked their passions to a constant, frantic blaze. The illusion of vitality made them behave like the eager paramours they had been long ago, when the crickets had chirped, and the wind whispered of their love.

Like the sleeping brew, Murdina knew the effect would not last.

Soon Hendry would shed the glory of renewed love and return to wallowing in his endless hatred of druid and mortal kind. She would fare no better. Her sanity teetered on a thin ledge of late. One more blow would likely send her to the very bottom of the abyss, into that darkness that she would never again escape. She would lose her grip on the last shreds of her reason.

Hendry would have to kill her, and to do such a thing would surely end him.

The roil of Murdina's thoughts made her inch out of their bed, taking care not to disturb her beloved. She pulled on his robe, needing the scent of him on her flesh, and padded out of the cottage. In the frost-edged night she saw that the rim of the horizon had turned a dark violet, and the stars had begun to wink out. Most of their *caraidean* had positioned themselves around the settlement in their old places, where they had once stood as giant totems. Weakened by darkness, they waited for the dawn to bring the sunlight that would revitalize them. She envied them that ability. Nothing could vanquish the paralyzing, silent blackness that had swallowed her alive in Bhaltair Flen's stone prison.

The sun freed me. Mayhap I'm part famhair.

Murdina was amused by the ridiculous thought. Hendry and their *caraidean* believed her unaware of the true depth and breadth of her madness, when in fact it had been her constant companion since girlhood. Over these last weeks she'd learned that her particular lunacy could be comforting, even beautiful. Unbound by the restraints of reason, she could think and speak and act as her battered heart willed—as long as she still possessed some choice in the matter.

When that last dignity began to slip through her grasp, perhaps she would save Hendry the trouble and drown herself in the loch. That begged another question: as an immortal she could burn, but could she still drown?

Movement in the dead brush near her made Murdina go still. She peered through the shadows and saw broad shoulders and a head of mortal hair. Interested now, she watched him hurry out into the clearing, where the rising sun briefly illuminated his human features. He glanced around him before he dove into the ground and vanished.

Why does Ochd sneak away from the settlement?

Murdina knew she should go and wake Hendry, for the giant had no reason or orders to go off on his own. The more her lover altered Ochd's body and mind, the more like a human male he behaved. He no longer needed as much sun or rest as the other *famhairean*. Since the fire at the mill Ochd had also been pestering Hendry with his repeated requests to hunt down that dark wench, the one with the special talent.

Murdina smiled, smug that she had worked it out on her own. While the others slept Ochd must have been going off to search for Rowan. The ache of being parted from her surely drove him to it. Before becoming Hendry's lover Murdina had secretly followed her beloved everywhere. Even in her younger years being near him had quieted the voices from within that had never ceased taunting her. He'd made her feel the only hope of happiness she'd ever known.

That Ochd might be equally enchanted by the wench only proved that their plan would work beautifully—as long as Hendry felt he had the altered *famhair* under his control. She knew how important it was for her lover to believe he held sway over them all.

I shall fetch back the lad, and no one shall be the wiser.

Silently Murdina retrieved her boots from the cottage, and then went into the woods where the clumsy Tri had been sent to guard nothing at all. She'd always felt kinship with the mind-damaged giant, now in his third or fourth body after his perpetual blunders had destroyed all his previous forms. What none of the other *caraidean* seemed to realize was that with a little patience and proper diversion Tri could be made quite useful.

"'Tis morning, Tri," she called to him as she reached up to touch his stiff face.

On either side of the split in his face his eyes opened, and his mouth stretched into a jagged caricature of a grin. "Lady."

"We shall play a game. Dinnae speak until I give you leave." She took him by the hand like a bairn, and led him out to the furrow in the soil where Ochd had disappeared. "Can you follow this path underground to where it leads? And take me with you?"

He nodded, hoisted her into his arms, and pressed her face against the ragged tunic he wore. The strong resinous smell of him came through the wool and almost choked Murdina, but she kept her nose and mouth against the fabric as he jumped into the ground.

Frozen soil and cold stone exploded around them as Tri burrowed through the earth. The heat of his body intensified as he did, and soon a heavy layer of mud coated them both. Keeping her eyes closed and holding her breath, Murdina suddenly thought of Hendry waking alone in their cottage. How frantic he would be once he discovered her gone. She would have to be quick with collecting Ochd and bringing him back with Tri. Perhaps in the process she would learn something that could please her lover, such as where the Skaraven had been keeping the troublesome wenches.

Just as Murdina began to feel dizzy from lack of air, Tri surfaced and placed her on her feet. She wiped the accumulated muck from her face and saw they stood a short distance from another furrow. Tri clumsily tried to rub off the mud clinging to her, and at the same time gave her a pleading look.

"You may whisper," Murdina told him.

"Ochd go there." He pointed past the other furrow to the outer wall of a stronghold. "We go, play game?"

"Soon, my friend. You stay here and watch for Ochd. Dinnae return to the settlement without me." Murdina waited for him to nod before she made her way toward the edge of the trees.

The castle beyond the outer wall looked very large and well-built. Many large mortal men with swords stood guard at the entries, and more patrolled in pairs outside the walls. Murdina heard approaching horses, and turned her head to see two clansmen on horseback escorting a dark-robed druid riding a much smaller pony. When he pulled back his hood to reveal his old, tired face she saw he had piercing dark eyes.

"Fair morning, Master Flen," one of the sentries called as he walked out from the gatehouse. "The laird shall be pleased to see you."

"I doubt that, lad," Bhaltair said as he slowly dismounted. "Naught 'tis more annoying than being dragged from bed by an untimely visitor."

Murdina shook with the rage that promptly swelled up inside her. The hateful old fool who had ruined her existence now stood making jests, as if he hadn't a care in the world. He'd stolen her freedom, imprisoned her in frozen darkness, and left her to rot beside Hendry. Her lips peeled back with a snarl as she remembered how it had been for them, to be so close and yet unable to touch each other.

For that and all they had suffered, Murdina would tear out Bhaltair Flen's throat with her teeth.

She summoned all her magic as she ran for the old druid, her boots gouging out chunks of muddy snow from the ground. In another moment she would be on him, and her protective body wards would keep the mortals at bay while she did her work. She'd take one of their swords and chop off Flen's head as a trophy for Hendry–

Hard hands snatched Murdina by the waist, one clamping over her mouth and nose as Ochd dragged her back behind a wide tree trunk. There he held her struggling body back against him until lack of air made her vision dim.

Ochd leaned out far enough to look at the stronghold before he eased his grip enough for her to heave in a breath. "You shouldnae have come here, Mistress."

Murdina opened her mouth to order him to release her, and heard a bone crack as scorching agony lanced through her jaw and cheek. The moment she cried out Ochd covered her mouth again and tucked her under his arm. He carried her deeper into the trees, stopping when he saw Tri waiting by the furrows.

"You brought her here?" Ochd demanded.

"Aye. Murdina, me play game," the damaged giant said. "Find you."

"So you have. Take her back to the settlement, and bring her to Hendry," Ochd said, ignoring her renewed struggles. "She has hurt her jaw and needs tending."

Tri cocked his scarred head. "Finish game. You chase."

Murdina groaned against Ochd's hand as the other giant dove into the furrow and tunneled out of the forest. His split face popped out of the ground a short distance from a patrol, who drew their swords and bellowed to the other guards.

Tri's grin faded as he saw the clansmen running toward him, and he dropped back into the furrow. Emerging beside Ochd and Murdina, he said, "Mortals no' play."

"Follow us," Ochd told him, and then

turned Murdina to face him. "I didnae intend to hurt you, my lady."

She spat in his face, sending a new jolt of agony through her jaw. A moment later the world went dark and hard and cold as the *famhair* took her down into the earth.

Murdina came in and out of awareness as her body became slick with muck. Holding her breath made her dizzy, and her broken jaw grew hard and heavy. By the time Ochd surfaced she heard a wretched mewling sound, and realized it came from her own throat.

Fierce hands wrenched her away from the famhair, and then Hendry's face appeared above hers.

"Sweetness mine," he murmured, cradling her against his chest as he kissed her brow. "What happened to you? Who hurt you?"

Murdina tried to tell him, but the muffled, ugly sounds grating from her lips wouldn't form the words. She rolled her eyes toward Ochd and Tri, who hovered on her other side.

"I didnae take Murdina from you, Hendry," Ochd said quickly. "I went to the midlands alone. Your lady and Tri followed me."

"No, we play game," Tri said, looking confused. "Wood Dream say chase Ochd. Then Ochd break lady's face."

"I meant only to keep her quiet, to protect her from the mortals near us," the other giant protested. "I reckoned her body shield would protect her—"

"No' against your altered form," Hendry said. "Aon." When the leader of the *famhairean* appeared, Hendry lifted Murdina into his arms. "Take her to the cottage and give her some poppy juice. Send the others to draw water from the loch for heating. I'll have to bathe her after I bind her jaw."

Murdina saw the look in Hendry's eyes, and shook her head, groaning as more pain stabbed through her face. If he gave into his fury he might turn their *caraidean* against them, and that would put an end to all their plans.

"Never worry, beloved mine," her lover told her, and gestured for the giant to take her away.

She looked past Aon's arm, and saw the air around Hendry begin to shimmer. The other *famhairean* also noticed and knew what it meant, for they began moving away from the druid and the two giants.

"You made me thus," Ochd said, reaching out to her lover. "You ken that I would never harm the Wood Dream."

"Yet you did. As they did. As the world did. She's the mind of a bairn and you hurt her." Hendry lifted his hands, which took on an amber-red glow. *"I willnae have it."*

The power that poured from his palms rammed into Ochd and Tri, whose bodies exploded like lightning-struck trees. Smoldering splinters of their forms rained down all around Hendry, who watched the two *famhairean's* spirits rise from the scorched marks the blast had left on the barren ground.

As Aon carried Murdina into the cottage, she realized at last that she was not alone in her madness.

Chapter Ten

THE SHOCK OF learning they'd traveled even further back in time at first made Emeline sit down on one of the stone benches and retreat into silence. How could she manage in a time two thousand years before her own? She knew almost nothing about the era or the people. Her country hadn't even been named Scotland yet. In school she'd been more interested in the sciences and had paid very little attention to her classes in ancient history. All she could remember about this century was that the Roman Empire ruled the world, Pompeii had blown up, and Christianity had begun.

They might as well have landed on Mars.

She heard water splashing, and watched

Ruadri wash his hands before he dampened one of the rough cloths and brought it to her.

"Permit me?" he asked, and when she nodded he slipped the cool, wet cloth under her hair, and pressed it against her nape.

Emeline felt immediate relief from the heat and sweat that had collected under the heavy mass of her hair.

"'Twill be cooler when the sun sets," the shaman told her.

He didn't seem to be bothered by the fact that they'd gone so far back in time. "How can you be so calm about this?"

"You're healed," Ruadri said. "'Tis enough for me."

She grimaced, a bit chagrined by the reminder. The shaman rose and moved to the center of the *broch*, where he knelt and murmured something. He had to be speaking an early form of Gaelic, judging by some of the word sounds. What he said could have been profanity, poetry or prayer, but it wouldn't get them out of this mess.

If they really were in the first century, then they'd been completely removed from every hope of help they had. What if the tribe decided they were enemies? As an immortal Ruadri could probably survive anything, but a simple spear jab would finish her.

Rays of sunlight slowly wandered from one side of the dirt floor to the other as Emeline considered and discarded every other possible explanation. Ruadri and his clan had once lived in this time, so he would recognize it. The tribesmen, the strange countryside, the *brochs*—everything supported his claim. But why would the portal carry them back another twelve centuries when the shaman had meant to send her to the future?

As the light faded Ruadri came to crouch before her again.

"Dinnae be fearful," he said, his deep voice so soft it made her feel as if she were being caressed. "I reckon that the portal brought us to this time for some purpose. We've only to fathom it."

That revelation made her stiffen. "The portals can do that? Act on their own? Move people to any point in time?"

"No' by chance." He moved to sit beside her. "I ken 'tis troubling, but 'tis done by the hand of the Gods. We mustnae doubt their purpose."

Emeline looked down at her hand, which he'd taken in his. No wonder he was so calm. His faith poured through her like a sparkling fountain of liquid crystal. Ruadri believed everything he said. A long time ago she'd felt the same trust in the God her parents had worshipped. What she'd seen as a nurse had worn away most of her faith, but she'd still tried to follow the teachings of the church, and live a good, decent life, until she'd come here.

Panic jolted through her. "Am I the reason this happened? Did it send us back here because of what I did?"

"Never, lass. You did naught wrong." He put his arm around her, tucking her against his side, and stroked the length of her hair. "The sacred grove wouldnae heal your affliction only to punish you for suffering it."

That seemed logical. She also knew from experience that the portals contained enormous and mysterious powers. But could these time travel conduits also be intelligent, and capable of independent thought and actions?

"If we were sent here for a purpose," she said slowly, reaching to scratch her itching side, "then why don't we know what it is?"

"I dinnae ken, but 'twill be made clear." He shifted to look at her side. "What plagues you? No' the spear wound, surely."

She pulled up the hem of her tunic to see the now-unnecessary sutures sticking out of her smooth flesh. "It's gone, but it seems that your Gods left in the stitches. May I borrow your dagger?"

"Will you allow me to remove them?"

When she nodded Ruadri eased her down on her side, and then drew the blade from his boot. He honed the edge on the side of the stone bench before he began neatly slicing through the knotted loops. One by one he quickly tugged out the bits of thread, until all that remained were two rows of tiny punctures.

She couldn't have done such a neat job of it, Emeline thought, and wondered why she had ever doubted his proficiency as a healer. He'd been so gentle she'd barely felt his fingers, and yet the heat of longing raced up her throat and into her face. What would it feel like to have those strong, skillful hands touch her everywhere?

Now is not the time to daydream about getting up to no good with the shaman.

"Thank you," Emeline said, bracing her hands as she started to sit up.

"Be still yet, lass" Ruadri told her as he opened a pouch and removed a corked stone vial. From it he dribbled some drops of thick golden liquid and smeared them over the little wounds.

The scent told her what it was. "Does the honey keep it from infecting?"

"Aye." He replaced the vial's cork. "And 'tis more pleasing to a lady's nose than my yarrow salve. Why do you call yourself fat?"

The unexpected question startled a laugh out of her. "I am. Just look at me."

Ruadri frowned. "I cannae see it."

Emeline glanced down to point out the obvious curve of her belly, but saw that it had vanished. Along with a flat abdomen, she had a new, narrower waist. She could even see the faint outlines of her lower ribs.

"I didn't realize I'd lost so much weight." That sounded ridiculous, so she added, "They didn't give us enough food, and even when they did I couldn't eat much with my bruised jaw. They never let us bathe. I suppose I was so busy looking after the others I didn't notice it."

"Even starved you're fetching, lass." He tugged down her tunic and helped her stand. "But you mustnae call yourself such names."

"I suppose you'd rather have me fat?" She cringed at the unconscious innuendo. "I didn't mean that."

Ruadri settled his hands on her waist, and the amber torrents of his desire wrapped around her. "I'd have you whatever your shape. You've a lovely body, Emeline, but 'tis no' what pulls me to you. Your spirit calls to mine. The moon marked you for me."

Was he going to kiss her again? He wanted to. So much so that she could already feel the tingle of it on her own lips.

"Why did you call me your *bhean*?"

The door covering rustled as Drest walked in and eyed them. "Your pardon, Shaman. The tribe gathers now for the meal."

Ruadri didn't release her as he nodded to the tribesman, who just as quickly withdrew. "I shall explain later. Only ken that Ara willnae speak directly to you before his tribe," he said, keeping his voice low. "None of the men shall, but 'tis no' an insult. Pritani consider it unmannerly to offer more than a greeting to a female no' of the tribe."

Emeline's sensual daze vaporized. "So, I should keep quiet."

"They think us *dru-wids*, and ken them to be quiet folk. 'Tis expected you will speak only to me and do as I shall." He removed his tartan and wrapped it around her. "But should Ara's ladies ask of our journey, say naught of the time travel."

Ruadri escorted her on his arm out of the *broch* and followed the waiting Drest to the center of the settlement. There the tribe had gathered in small groups around a huge fire now burning in the stone-lined pit, in which large iron and stone pots had been nestled. The scent of roasting meat and fish blended with a sharp, sweet smell that Emeline guessed was some sort of ale. She saw the men passing around oddly-shaped skin bags and drinking from their gathered spouts. Sleepy-eyed infants in fur slings nursed or slept on their mother's breasts, while their older siblings sat cross-legged on the ground. Everyone had small, rough wooden trenchers near them, but no one had begun eating.

Ara rose from the bench placed near the fire and beckoned to them. "Come, sit with me and mine, Tree-Knowers."

Although the gathering seemed bucolic, Emeline saw every man had armed himself with clubs, blades and even a few scary-looking axes. A few men stood away from the fire looking to the south, each holding a spear in hand. It looked as if the tribe expected to be attacked, but not perhaps by her or Ruadri.

Once they sat on the benches brought for them, an older, heavily-tattooed tribesman with silvered black hair stood and lifted his arms.

"'Tis the tribe's shaman," Ruadri murmured to her.

Everyone fell silent and watched as the shaman offered thanks to the Gods. Emeline found the prayer he offered fascinating. He considered everything from the summer's bounty to the good health of their children as divine gifts. It seemed a little effusive, as

they had obviously done all the work to care
and provide for their families. Yet from the
appreciative emotions glowing around her
she knew they believed even their abilities
came from the Gods. Such grateful devotion
stirred something in her that she hadn't felt
since she'd lost her parents. Emeline had
been so resentful and envious of what she
couldn't have that she'd forgotten her own
blessings.

Surviving being thrown back through
time, weeks of abuse and neglect, and her own
gift turning on had been miraculous. She had
four strong, admirable women who had
become her first and only true friends. Then
there was Ruadri, who had only tried to help
her. Even after she'd treated him horribly, and
tried to kill Rowan, he refused to give up on
her. He'd defied his chieftain's orders to try to
heal her, and hadn't blamed her for landing
them here, in this strange place and time.

Emeline had never once offered him a
word of thanks for any of it.

When the prayer of gratitude ended all of
the tribe echoed the shaman's last words—
mòran taing—she looked at Ruadri as she

murmured the same in modern English to him.

"Many thanks."

His mouth flattened. "Save them, lass. I've done little enough, and badly at that."

Ara made an encompassing gesture toward the fire, and both men and women began portioning out the food in the trenchers. Emeline liked that they served the elderly and the children first, even before their chieftain. Drest and several hard-looking warriors helped the women cut up food and feed the youngest, making it clear that tending to toddlers was not beneath them. She did notice that Ara sat alone, and wondered if the headman had lost his wife. There seemed to be very few elderly people among the tribe.

A slim young boy brought two trenchers and placed them in front of Ruadri, directing an openly admiring look at Emeline as he did.

Ara chuckled as the boy hurried off to join a group of other adolescents. "Your shy *bhean* snares hearts young and old, Shaman."

Emeline was glad it was dark, to hide her reddening face as she sampled a piece of smoked fish.

"'Tis how she caught mine," Ruadri said as he regarded her. "One look and I became hers."

"'Tis the fate of the moon-ridden to serve a waking goddess," the chieftain said, nodding at the tattoos on his forearms. "She's built for many strong bairns. Be you yet so blessed?"

Ruadri shook his head. "We mated but winter last."

Emeline was confused by what he'd said. Did he mean the mark on her ankle? No, she vaguely remembered Althea telling her how she'd been mated to Brennus. Although they hadn't had a ceremony yet Cadeyrn already referred to Lily as his mate. In the fourteenth century mate meant wife or husband.

Ruadri was saying they were married?

Barely avoiding choking on the fish, Emeline swallowed a few times before she gratefully accepted a wooden cup from a woman sitting beside her. It contained some sort of cider that tasted sharp and pulpy, but she swallowed a mouthful.

Of course, he was lying about it, but why would he say such a thing? Did an unmarried man and woman traveling together violate some sort of Pritani taboo? But Ara didn't think they were Pritani. He believed them to both be druids. Or had she misinterpreted that, too?

"We seek a *dru-wid* tribe of the forest," Ruadri was saying now. "'Tis no' far from here to their settlement. Ken you the Wood Dream?"

"Aye." The chieftain's stern expression softened. "Good folk they be. We trade often." He turned to Drest. "How fared the Wood Dream on last your visit?"

"Thriving as ever," his son replied. "Gardens and pens near bursting full. Their headman offered ten sows for our white mare. I refused."

Ara grunted. "Well you did, for she's worth thirty." He regarded the shaman. "You've Wood Dream kin?"

"Old friends we wish to visit for solstice," Ruadri said. "We go to them after the meal."

"Travel through a storm, and the Sluath shall take you as their slaves forever," the chieftain said, pointing to dark clouds toward the east. "You're blood-kin by bond. Shelter here the night, then go at dawn."

Emeline watched Ruadri's guarded features as he considered Ara's offer. She knew Hendry and Murdina had belonged to the Wood Dream tribe, and that the *famhairean* had been created after the Romans had massacred their people. Yet Drest had just said that the tribe was thriving.

That's because the massacre hasn't happened yet.

Emeline felt a little dizzy as she realized why Ruadri had asked about the druid settlement. If they could warn the Wood Dream tribe of the impending slaughter, the tribe could then avoid it by abandoning their settlement and hiding somewhere until the Romans passed through their lands. If the tribe survived, their totems would never evolve into the *famhairean*. Hendry and Murdina would have no reason to be imprisoned or seek vengeance against druid kind.

They could save everyone in the future and the past, right here and now.

"I wouldnae impose, but my bond urges me to accept." Ruadri lifted her hand to his lips, and when he met her gaze she nodded quickly. "I must keep safe my *bhean*."

The words came with a swirling sensation

of tangerine heat throbbing so deep inside Emeline she thought she'd burst into flames. The shaman's emotions couldn't have been more clear, and answered the question she'd asked before leaving the *broch*.

Tonight, she would be his.

Chapter Eleven

꧁꧂

FTER FINISHING THEIR
evening meal, the tribe let the fire
die down, and couples began
carrying off their sleepy-eyed children to their
beds. While Ara and Ruadri talked about
trade and horses Emeline went to help the
women collecting the trenchers. She saw the
chieftain watching her, and belatedly realized
that visitors probably weren't expected to help
with the clean-up. Since she'd already made
the mistake, she followed the women to a
small stream nearby the village. There she
watched for a moment until she saw how they
scoured the wooden dishes clean with sand
and water. Rolling up her sleeves, she knelt
down to help.

"You neednae do washing, *Dru-widess*," a worried-looking woman said to her. "You be visitor."

"She be Ara's blood," the oldest, a stout female with pure white hair, told her. "His *máthair* didnae tip her nose at work. The lass be the same." She turned to give Emeline a measuring look. "What do you for your tribe, Daughter?"

She glanced back at Ruadri, who looked deep in conversation with Ara and the tribe's shaman. Her shared blood wasn't giving her the word for nurse, or even a hint as to whether female caregivers in this time were called healers. At last she went with a description.

"I attend to our elders."

Every woman stopped washing and looked at her.

"*All* your elders, lady?" one asked faintly.

Emeline wondered what they thought she meant. "Aye, when they be sick or injured."

Some of the youngest giggled until the white-haired woman gave them a narrow look. "Still your tongues. Our ways arenae as the *dru-wid*. Her *sheshey* sits among us, and his eyes dinnae meander."

"To wish that they would, Marga," a beautiful redhead said, and released a dreamy sigh. "I'd attend a grand, fetching man as he from morn to moon."

"Keep to your own," Marga said, sounding stern now. "'Tis wise to provide for the sickly old. We be closer to the ears of the Gods, and ken your names."

That silenced the mirth, and most of the other women looked almost embarrassed. The redhead collected some trenchers and hurried back to the fire.

"Give them no heed," the white-haired woman told Emeline. "Your goodness be plain."

She didn't feel especially good, not with all the wicked thoughts she'd had about Ruadri. Without warning a very small girl rushed past her chasing a firefly and slipped on the wet bank. Emeline lunged for her, catching her up in her arms and dragging her away from the edge of the stream.

"Careful, little one," she said, and handed

the now wailing child to the white-faced young woman who rushed at her with open arms.

The mother gripped Emeline's shoulder tightly before she carried off her toddler. While all the other women made sharp trilling sounds, Marga clasped her hands and said, "What be seen be truth."

Emeline was confused. "I didnae wish her to fall in."

"Aye, and show yourself to all." The older woman leaned closer and lowered her voice. "Only you must eat more, Daughter, and make yourself more abundant. You've beauty, but you've near worn yourself to bone. Men desire feast, no' famine."

Being regarded as beautiful and too thin was a first for Emeline, and for a moment she wondered if the old lady had trouble with her eyes. Then she noticed that almost all of the women had sumptuous, curvy bodies that would definitely be considered overweight in her time. None of them seemed bothered by their ample sizes, and most had sewn their garments to hug their full breasts and wide hips.

Compared to them she actually did look scrawny.

Washing out the trenchers properly took some time, but once they had been scrubbed the women carried them back to the village and stacked them around the pit stones to dry. As they finished the task together the women nodded to Emeline, and a few touched her arm or shoulder as they murmured their thanks.

"For you, Daughter," Marga said, and offered Emeline a length of cord with a small polished stone hanging from it. On the stone a tiny, antlered deer had been carved and painted in white. "We see you now."

"This…'Tis lovely," Emeline said.

"'Tis our sacred stag," the older woman said. "Like the moon he changes, yet he be watchful over our tribe. So over you on your travels."

"My thanks."

As she tied the necklace around her neck Emeline felt a curious sensation of stillness inside her, as if she were standing in the moonlight atop a high plateau. The feeling drifted like falling snow through her from throat to ankle, making her glance down. A patch of pale light shimmered on the side of her boot before it faded away.

She turned to rejoin Ruadri and the chieftain, only to bump into the shaman's chest. When he lifted his hands to steady her, she thought she saw a shimmer run through the tattoos on his forearms.

Marga went to the headman and tucked her arm through his as she murmured to him. Then out loud she said, "She's blood-kin, *Sheshey*. As gentle and fair as your *máthair*. With no thought she saved a bairn from the stream." Her expression turned a little smug as she said to Emeline, "Ara be my mate."

She'd just been put through some sort of subtle test, Emeline thought, and couldn't help grinning back at the sly old lady.

"You be kin to my tribe through your *bhean*, Shaman," Ara said, and bowed to Emeline. "Ever be you welcome among us. Fair night."

Emeline dropped into a somewhat wobbly curtsey, and then watched with Ruadri as the chieftain took Marga's arm and walked into the shadows. "He really means that, doesn't he?"

"My cleverest words didnae impress him half so much as your aid with the washing and the opinions of his wife." He smiled down at her. "Pritani men treasure their families, and anyone who shows them such kindness. But 'tis the headwoman who has the final word."

That reminded her. "We need to talk about some things."

Ruadri led her back to the visitor's *broch*, where someone had left several new rushlights burning for them. As he'd predicted, the interior had cooled with the onset of evening. Carefully he replaced the wooden wedges in the narrow window openings.

"Now we may speak openly," he said quietly.

She didn't want to press the one big issue first. "Why did you ask Ara about the Wood Dream tribe?"

"Learning they yet lived made clear our purpose." He knelt and sketched a simple map in the dirt floor to show her the relative position of the druid's settlement, which appeared to be due south of Ara's village. "Tomorrow

I'll water-travel from the stream to the Wood Dream's loch and warn them of the coming attack."

So, he had come to the same conclusion, she thought, feeling relieved. "Good. Now how is it that I understand the tribe's language?"

He looked as if he didn't want to tell her, and then he said, "Mayhap your druid blood remembers it. This tribe shall sire the McAra. They're your people. More I cannae tell you."

More like he didn't know what to tell her, Emeline sensed, but let it go. "Does *bhean* mean mate, or wife? As in we're married?" When he nodded she wanted to hit him. "Why in heaven's name would you tell them that?"

"For the same reason I didnae wish you to remain at Dun Mor," he said slowly. "An unmated female's fate belongs to her people's leader, whether he be the laird of the McAra, or the headman of this tribe. If Ara learns we arenae mated, he would take you from me and claim you as his property. With your coloring none would question it."

Emeline was taken aback. "Just because I look like them he can treat me like livestock?"

"No' in your era," Ruadri countered, and put his hands on her shoulders. "But in mine, and this time, aye. 'Tis the mortal custom, and meant to protect young females. I cannae change it, so I must keep the truth concealed until I can return you to the future."

So, he didn't want her as his mate or to stay. Her stomach dropped and a familiar ache filled her chest as she backed away from him. At least it was out in the open.

"We'd better get some sleep," she muttered. She glanced over at the furs piled on the sleeping platform. "I don't suppose you know a spell for making an extra bed."

"The nights grow cold even in midsummer," Ruadri said. "You'll be warmer if we share it."

Emeline eyed him, but from the utter lack of emotions coming from him she knew he meant just what he said. He only wanted to keep warm. That left her to be the awkward, embarrassed one, as she was pretty sure she wouldn't sleep at all cuddled up with him.

"Give me some of the furs and I'll sleep on the floor."

"Dinnae be foolish, Emeline." Now he sounded annoyed.

Making a fuss about sleeping with him probably was petty, but she'd had enough of pretense for one night.

"It's fine," she assured him as she marched over to grab some of the furs. "I've always slept alone."

Ruadri took the furs out of her hands and tossed them back on the bed. "You've naught to dread from me. I would but lay beside you, my lady."

"Of course you would."

She must have imagined the fiery-hot desire he'd felt before. Or worse, he'd been feeling it for one of the other women. *What would Ara make of that,* she thought as she glared up at him.

"You shouldn't call me your lady. You shouldn't have kissed me and said all those things to me. You shouldn't have made me believe that you meant them. But I suppose I made it easy for you. I'm a virgin, and no man has ever wanted me. Not seriously. I wouldn't know any better."

As soon as the last words spilled from her lips Emeline sank down on the bed and buried her face in her hands. How could she have told him that? She pressed her fingertips against her eyelids, praying they'd hold back her tears of humiliation.

A roaring tidal wave of liquid crimson heat slammed over her a heartbeat before Ruadri dragged her off the bed and into his arms. Her feet left the floor as he lifted her to his eye level, the flickering rushlights lashing his face with gold and black. His eyes gleamed like melting silver, and in them she saw a hunger so ferocious it should have terrified her.

"I've no' wanted anything as much as you," he said, pressing her body to his so she could feel the knots of his muscles, and the swollen thickness of his erection. "I look upon you and see every dream of my life. Hopes I've no' dared to have."

Emeline felt as if her bones had liquefied. "I'm only a woman, Ruadri."

"You're more than I've words to say. I look upon you and see paradise. I put my hands on you and my blood turns to flame. 'Twas good that you told me no' to touch you when you first came to me. If you hadnae, I'd have taken you to my bed and made you mine." He dragged in a breath. "And you tell me you're untouched, as if 'twere shameful. To ken that you're yet a maiden, that I might be yours before any other…"

Her virginity didn't repel him. He saw it as a gift. Emeline knew one thing: she was never going back to the twenty-first century.

"So, don't make me cry again." She looped her arms around his neck. "Make me your woman."

"Thank the Gods," he murmured as he set her down.

The rushlights had begun to burn low, which helped when he began undressing her. As she did the same for him she thought her hands would fumble with shyness. The more she exposed his huge, tough body, however, the more assured she felt. When her fingers stroked over the plains and hills of his muscles, his chest rumbled with sounds of low, deep pleasure. The slide of her body against his made her go instantly, completely wet. In her belly a huge rose of delight bloomed, caressing her with velvety petals of promised delight and pricking her with sharp thorns of urgent need.

"Dinnae fear me, lass," Ruadri said when she shivered.

Emeline pressed her bare breasts against his chest, sighing as his smooth flesh caressed the pebbly peaks. "This isn't fear."

Ruadri's feelings grew hotter and darker, filling her like a steaming waterfall of burgundy wine. She'd never once gotten drunk, but she knew this must be what it felt like. As his hands splayed across her lower back her skin turned to silk under his touch, and she poured her delight into him so he could feel her soft, feminine pleasure. He took off his boots before he sat her on the edge of the platform to remove hers, and then they were both naked and stretched out facing each other on the furs.

His closeness, and the cool air against Emeline's heated skin, made her more aware of her body than she'd ever been. She felt delicate and decadent, and the scent of their bodies blended into an arousing musk. The flickering lights hid as much as they revealed, and she wondered what it would be like to lay naked with Ruadri in a sunlit meadow.

Could I let him see every inch of me like that? Her heart said *yes* and *please* and *tomorrow, as soon as we're alone.*

She wanted to see all of him, too, Emeline decided, although she sensed that no man in any time had ever looked as magnificent as her shaman. But what he felt for her was remaking her from the inside, already changing her perceptions from that of a lonely spinster to a vibrant woman.

Something other than her charms, however, made heavy ropes of pewter doubt crisscross through his flowing desire. He also wasn't touching her.

"You don't have to worry about me," she assured him. "I know how this happens, at least from medical books. And I'm really not afraid."

"'Tis me, no' you. I've never put my hands on a lass in passion." He caressed her shoulder, and then drew his palm down the length of her arm, so gently that she barely felt it. "I dinnae wish to hurt you."

No wonder he had doubts. As big and powerful as he was, he could probably snap her bones by simply holding her too tight. Her utter lack of experience and the physical reality of her virginity wouldn't make taking him easy or painless, either. But Ruadri wasn't a brute, and she refused to be a coward.

"Then you've only to do one thing." She pressed her hand to his cheek, her lips to his mouth, and his hand to her heart. "Take me now."

Chapter Twelve

ISSING RUADRI WHILE she pushed her breast into his palm had to be the brashest thing Emeline had ever done. Encouraging him to caress her made her feel wild and shameless, and shattered the weighty restraints damming his need. He clasped her mound as he ravished her mouth, sending explosions of aching sweetness through her. His hand draped her thigh over his, and she pressed close until she could feel the hard length of him against her folds. His penis was huge, but she had grown so slick with desire that she was sure she drenched him at the first touch.

"I'm starved for you, lass," he said against

her lips, his massive frame tensing before he shifted down.

The feel of his mouth nuzzling her breasts made her surge against him, stroking the long, hard column between her legs with her eager, slick folds. But rocking against him wasn't enough, not when he began sucking her nipples. He licked and tugged until she thought she would shake herself to pieces. At last she hitched her thigh higher and reached between them, boldly curling her fingers around his pulsing shaft.

As she notched his satiny cockhead into the aching opening of her pussy, Ruadri shuddered. "Ah, Gods. I should wait…"

"Not another moment," she whispered, pressing him in. "Come inside me, please."

He rolled over her, pinning her down under his weight, his hands dragging her thighs around his hips. He stayed lodged just inside her, his whole body tightening as he looked into her eyes. He looked like a warrior about to conquer, and a boy receiving his most secret wish. Those two sides of him both came into her, hunger and longing like armies marching under the banner of love.

"Always you'll be mine, Emeline." He pushed into her, his girth stretching her slowly as he penetrated and claimed her.

The pain she had expected flared with every inch of him she took, but the delicious cascade of his fervent emotions soon washed it away. Ruadri might have drowned her in his need, but she poured into him her own yearning, and together they merged in a dark, wild sea of emotion. All around him her body softened and clenched at the same time, until he groaned and pushed one hand under her bottom, gripping her tightly. She arched up, engulfing him to his root, and her breath mingled with his as they both let out a heartfelt sigh.

Moving from innocence to womanhood infused Emeline with an insatiable delight. She had taken all of him, and they fit together as if made for each other. Her own strong frame braced him without the slightest difficulty, and for the first time in her life she felt right in her own body.

"Ruadri." She slid her hands over his back, glorying in the feel of the smooth flesh over his bunched muscles. "I didn't know it would be like this. Like you're part of me."

"'Tis more, my sweet lass." He gave her another of his possessive, hungry kisses.

Emeline gasped against his mouth as he moved, drawing out his length almost entirely before pushing back inside. The way his swollen cock stroked her made tremors surge through her belly and into her jutting breasts. The heat of that luscious friction spread in thrilling bursts of sensation unlike anything she'd ever experienced.

"Oh," she gasped.

When the flare of his glans grazed over a pulsating spot inside her it was as if he'd set off a pleasure charge that pervaded her with bursts of electrified sweetness.

"So much more," he said, his voice thick.

He slipped one hand between them, pressed his thumb to the top of her sex, and rubbed it against the tight pearl of her clit.

Emeline shivered, and then whimpered as he kept stroking her there while he worked his thick penis in and out of her. She had rubbed herself there before, furtively in her lonely bed at night, while imagining a man loving her.

Never had it felt like the reality of Ruadri touching her and taking her, and it excited her so much that everything inside her knotted.

"You make me want more even now," he murmured as he circled and caressed the hard knot, pressing deep into her softness. "I shall have you again with my mouth." He swept his thumb back and forth while he slowly pumped his shaft in and out. "I want to fack you with my fingers, my tongue. I'll devour you until you beg me put my cock in your quim and stroke you hard."

Her face burned and her body shook as Emeline writhed under him, and then he pushed hard into her pussy and tenderly squeezed her clit. The double stimulation excited her so much she came apart under him. His mouth muffled her cry, her body stretching and then shaking beneath his, as sensual bliss swamped her. The climax seemed to go on and on as he stroked her and fucked her and murmured to her how much she pleased him with her ecstasy.

"Oh, Ru." She finally went limp, exhausted, and entirely elated. If he'd never touched another woman in passion, how could

he already know her body so well? "What are
you doing to me?"

He kept gliding in and out of her. "Everything I've longed to, my lady. I've thought on
you like naught else. 'Tis so much yet."

She'd forgotten that in a way she was his
first too. Her heart fluttered in her breast as
she watched his eyes darken, and his expression tightened as if he were fighting for self-
control. All this time he had been seeing to her
needs while denying his own, and now he was
swelling even larger and harder inside her, and
still he held back.

That he wanted her so much and could
still be so gentle with her made Emeline blink
quickly. At last something she'd never understood became clear: this man was who she had
waited for. He was the reason she'd never
taken a lover.

"You don't have to wait any longer,"
Emeline murmured, and on instinct stretched
out her arms over her head. "Give me all of
you now."

Ruadri closed his eyes for a moment, and
when he looked at her again his eyes had
turned silver-white. He dragged up her legs

and plowed into her with a fierce stroke that sent a fiery shockwave through her. Before she could catch her breath, he did it again, and she gripped the furs with tight fingers as she lifted her hips into his powerful thrusts.

His forearm tattoos had begun to shimmer with light, and Emeline felt a strange tingle in the crescent scar on her ankle. Somehow that felt as right as Ruadri's savage passion, and she gave herself up to both as the light sank into her and filled her along with him.

The rushlights faded as the dark interior of the *broch* turned bright. As if from a distance Emeline saw chunks of wood flying through the air around them, and moonlight pouring in through the window openings. It curtained them with fountaining swirls of gray and white, circling and contracting until a thousand tiny moons filled the air.

A bolt of power raced from her ankle to her chest, where it swelled inside her and poured out through her skin to envelop them both. A new presence took her, but unlike the ugly darkness this was pure and beautiful. Emeline surrendered to it as she had to

Ruadri, and looked at her lover with so much joy she thought she might weep.

The shaman held himself deep inside her as the power enclosing them grew bright. Then Emeline cried out as pleasure suffused and shook her, and he swelled and jetted in her core. The bliss became so intense she thought her heart would explode, and then at last he shuddered and poured his last stream into her, and they both went limp.

"Long I've awaited this night, my warrior." The voice coming from her lips sounded like music over the rasp of her panted breathing. "You and your lady be one now. I've marked you, and I shall take my pleasure of you every night hence."

Ruadri went still, lifted his head to look at her through narrowed eyes. "Aye, Goddess, so you shall. But Emeline doesnae belong to you. She gave herself to me. 'Tis I who shall serve you, no' her. Release her."

"Never would I clad your lady or you with any chain, my shaman." A sharp sensation bit into her side as the words left her, and Emeline touched the tender scar of the wound writhing on her skin. "That you shall do yourself."

Emeline heard herself laugh, and then the presence vanished entirely as the moons crowding around them burst and faded away. The air still crackled around them as if filled with magic, which made her feel oddly comforted. Some enormous thing beyond her understanding had just happened, but it had not been evil or destructive. She would swear to that.

"Emeline?" Ruadri cradled her face. "Come back to me, lass."

"I'm back. I never left." She flung her arms around his neck and held him close, grateful and strangely close to tears. "I'm sorry. I don't know what that… I didn't say those things. Something spoke through me."

"'Twas my battle spirit, the moon. She rode you." He lifted her from the furs, his hard cock still buried inside her, and held her close, resting his cheek against the top of her head. "I never reckoned she would try to claim you."

She already has, Emeline thought, but he sounded so grim she kept that notion to herself. "It felt startling, but she didn't hurt me."

"She wouldnae." Carefully he lifted her,

separating their bodies, and lowered her to the furs before stretching out beside her.

Emeline studied his expression, which had gone from taut satisfaction to shuttered anger. "Why would the moon, ah, ride me like that?"

"I dinnae ken. Mayhap I used you too crudely. I ken that I hurt you." He sounded disgusted with himself. "The druids feared the Skaraven too brutal to be trusted with their fragile bodies. 'Twas why they chained us to our beds before they'd permit a pleasure lass to attend to our needs."

That shocked her down to her heels. "They put you in *chains*?"

Ruadri explained the only way the Skaraven had been permitted to have lovers, through an observed ritual during which they were chained and kept from touching or even speaking to the women brought to them for sex. Everything he described made her furious, for it seemed tantamount to rape. It also reduced what she now knew was a beautiful experience to shameful, deliberate humiliation.

"You didn't deserve that kind of abuse," Emeline told him once he'd finished. "What you and I did together wasn't crude or hurtful. There's almost always pain during a woman's first time. I expected that. But I am not fragile, and you are certainly not a brute. I couldn't have imagined it would be so thrilling. You might have to put *me* in chains the next time I..." She stopped as she remembered talking with Marga and the other tribeswomen.

Ruadri traced the down curve of her lips. "What makes you frown, then, lass?"

"Is 'attend' a term the Pritani use for having sex?" When he nodded Emeline groaned. "I told Ara's ladies that I 'attended' to all of our tribe's elders. Don't laugh," she added when she saw Ruadri's lips twitch. "My McAra blood didn't warn me I'd called myself a besom."

"None could look upon you and think that." He kissed her brow and gazed into her eyes. "Your courage shines as bright as your beauty."

So did his honesty. Emeline was almost blinded by the clear, crisp blue sky that stretched inside her along with his beautiful emotions. She could see herself as he did now, and it humbled her, but she didn't deserve it.

"You should know that I'm not particularly brave," she said slowly. "Ask Cade. He'll tell you how much trouble I caused during the escape from the mill."

"Cade told us how you struggled," Ruadri countered. "You walked full leagues and climbed slopes with an ankle broken. You cared for Lily when she fell senseless. You stepped in front of a spear meant for Perrin."

"Most of that was stupidity, not valor. Especially getting hit by that spear." She paused, working up the nerve to tell him the rest. "Even before I came here I was full of envy and misery. I've never been thin or pretty or well-liked by other women, and it always hurt. I've wasted years hating myself when I might have enjoyed the blessings and advantages I did have."

"'Tis why you thought yourself fat," he said, and looked down the length of her body. "'Twas what they called you, no' what you were."

"What I was doesn't matter anymore." Emeline was a little surprised by how much she meant that. In her time Meribeth Campbell and Lauren Reid had defined who she was. Now she did that on her own. "Everything has changed, including me. You've come into my life and I want to be brave and beautiful for you."

Ruadri shifted onto his back and stared up at the roof beams. "That you shall be, with or without me." Finally he turned his head to look at her. "I truly meant only to keep you warm tonight."

"You did that." Emeline climbed on top of him, snuggling against his broad chest. "I expect I'll never feel cold again."

Chapter Thirteen

✿❀✿

MAKING THE QUICK jaunt to the McAra stronghold for Althea meant rising at dawn and going for a short, fast swim on horseback. Although immortality had given her the ability to water-travel like the Skaraven, it did nothing to keep her warm when she led her mare into the river and transformed. Now accustomed to being whisked through the icy currents by the bubbling light magic that surrounded her mistress's water-bonding form, the horse only snorted and waggled her head as they emerged from the loch.

Having the ability to freeze anything she touched didn't provide Althea with any particular immunity to cold either. If anything, she felt it more keenly. She smiled her gratitude to the McAra clansmen waiting with fur-lined cloaks on the banks, mainly because if she opened her mouth they'd only hear her teeth chattering.

Because apparently they both had ice for blood, Brennus and Kanyth disdained the cloaks and simply shook off like wet tigers.

"This is just so unfair," Althea said once she had wrapped up. "How can you guys be completely immune to freezing weather?"

The men exchanged an amused look before Kanyth said, "We werenae coddled against it."

They thought it was funny, but Althea's mood darkened. Bred as indentured warriors, the Skaraven had been conditioned to endure physical hardships from birth. Brennus rarely talked about it, but she'd picked up enough to know what they'd suffered. During the years of brutal training they'd had as boys the druids had probably marched them through blizzards and made them sleep on frozen lakes to build up their resistance to cold.

"When we see Bhaltair, can you shake some spells out of him?" she asked her husband. "He might know a drying charm or something else useful. It'll keep me from kicking him in that bad knee of his, too."

"I'll keep you warm, Wife." Brennus lifted her from her mare to his big stallion and settled her on his lap. "And cease your worrying on Emeline."

How the love of her life always knew what she was really thinking still mystified Althea. "I still think we should have gone down to check on her before we left. She was really in bad shape. Plus it's not called the 'fear pit' because you feel warm and fuzzy when you're in it."

"Ru shall keep close watch over her until our return," Brennus said before he looked over at the clan's weapons master. "Ka, ride aside us. I want no surprises."

"You and your suspicions," his half-brother chided as he collected the reins and trotted up with Althea's mount. "Old Flen willnae dare ambush us." He saw the chieftain's expression and sighed. "Very well, be an old wench who twice counts her every kernel at the miller's. As for me, I've grown very fond of certain druidesses." He winked at Althea.

"Stop trifling with mine." Brennus

wrapped his arms around her before he touched his boot heels to the stallion's sides. As soon as the clansman rode ahead out of earshot he said in a lower voice, "During this, Flen shall vie for control of the clan. 'Tis the tree-knowers' way, but I'm determined that he'll have naught of that. Any agreement made comes from my lips alone."

"So, you brought me along just to keep *you* warm?" Althea asked in her sweetest voice.

"He didnae bring me for that," Kanyth said, and stroked his chin. "Mayhap the laird needs new swords forged. Or if I'm no' needed at the anvil, I might flirt with some of his wenches."

"Aye, and the McAra shall have your baws skewered by his blade before you can steal a kiss," Brennus warned him. "Dinnae be fooled by the man's size. When it comes to his kin, he's as protective as a marten over new kits— with twice the teeth."

The analogy made the weapons master visibly shudder. "As you say, Brother."

The ride to the McAra stronghold thankfully took only a short time. When they came in sight of the outer walls Althea imagined the steaming hot bath the laird's wife would have ready in the guest chamber. Lady McAra always provided a tub large enough for them both to share as well, which made her the perfect hostess.

"Bren." Kanyth nodded toward a group of riders approaching the front of the stronghold. "There 'tis Flen on that pony."

A rumbling sound drew Althea's gaze in the opposite direction, and she saw a *famhair* and a strange man with a mud-covered woman. All three were running away from the stronghold through the trees.

"Brennus, over there," Althea said. As the trio passed through a patch of light, she saw the woman's features. "My God, I think that's Murdina with them."

The ground began to shake, and the stallion reacted by skittering into Kanyth's mount. Brennus pushed the horses apart, jerked her out of the saddle and planted her back on her mare.

"Ride to the castle," he told her, and shouted for the McAra as he drew his sword. Mounted clansmen rode after the chieftain and his brother as they streaked toward the trees.

Althea could obey her husband, or she could help take down the evil bitch who had tortured her and her friends. Without hesitation she wheeled the mare around to follow the men. By the time she caught up with Brennus the mad druidess and her cohorts had vanished.

"Will you never listen to me?" the chieftain demanded, seizing the reins from her.

"Think of it as me challenging you, without the beating part." She used his arm for leverage as she dismounted and strode over to the holes in the ground. All they'd left behind was a deep furrow in the earth that narrowed and dwindled before it disappeared altogether. The *famhairean* could move through the earth so fast by now they were probably halfway across Scotland. "How could they have known we'd come here?"

"They didnae." Brennus looked back at the stronghold. "I'll wager they came for Flen."

A bigger group of McAra clansmen on horseback, led by their diminutive laird, converged on them. Resplendent in dark sapphire silk and white lace, Maddock McAra's crystal blue eyes glittered with malice as he dismounted. Although Althea stood a head taller than the laird, he had the presence of a much larger man, particularly when he was angry.

"Laird McAra." Brennus offered his arm.

The laird clasped it briefly. "No' the fair morning I'd hoped, Chieftain." He sketched a perfect bow toward Althea. "But you dim the sun itself, my lady." His jaw tightened as he eyed the furrow. "I see overlarge badgers have been digging their setts on my land. Shall I send patrols, Brennus, or summon my best trackers?"

"'Twould do naught to pursue them, Maddock. They've gone deep and left no trace beyond what we see." Her husband gestured to his half-brother. "My weapons master and half-brother, Kanyth. Permit him to speak with your patrols before they ride out, so he might tell them of the water weakness."

"Aye, for if they've encamped on my lands, they'll be driven into the bottom of the facking loch," the laird said, putting a razor edge on every word.

"By both our clans, my lord," Kanyth said and gave Brennus a sharp look before he rode over to join the clansmen.

Althea suddenly worked out why Kanyth had come to their meeting with Bhaltair Flen. Brennus had a short, volcanic temper, and he'd always despised the old druid for trying to manipulate the Skaraven. When stirred up, Maddock McAra could be just as hot-headed. Her husband had been relying on his half-brother, who had a gift for dispelling tensions, to keep everyone in check.

So that's my job until Ka returns, Althea thought, and smiled at Maddock. "I've been looking forward to this visit. Your wife promised to show me the new addition you were building for her in the solar."

"Aye, and after you put that notion in her head she wouldnae leave me in peace until I did," Maddock said, sniffing and plucking at his cuff. "She's now all manner of potted weeds growing in that 'green house.' Come and see the harm you've done to my poor castle."

"You'll appreciate it more when your cook has fresh herbs in mid-winter," Althea told him as Brennus helped her back up onto her mare. "I brought some rosemary and thyme that I sprouted in ours."

A tight group of clansmen accompanied them to the stronghold, where they were ushered in under guard. More men stood in defensive positions around the great hall, their swords drawn and their expressions lethal. Of course, Maddock knew exactly how dangerous the *famhairean* were, and would do whatever was necessary to protect his family and kin, but these men hadn't just shown up in the last five minutes.

Brennus tensed beside her, and Althea saw why as Bhaltair Flen slowly approached them.

"'Tis good to see you again, my lady." With a small lurch the old druid turned to her husband and bowed. "My thanks for this invitation, Chieftain."

Brennus's nostrils flared, but all he said was, "We've much to discuss, but I must first see to my wife's comfort."

"Before you retire to your chambers, I wished to ask how fares the McAra healer,"

Bhaltair said quickly. "From the affliction
Ruadri described to me, she should be kept
isolated from the other ladies at Dun
Mor until–"

"You've a McAra at Dun Mor, Chieftain?"
a deceptively soft voice asked.

Althea swallowed a groan as the laird
appeared beside the old druid. She couldn't
believe that the one thing they'd wanted to
keep secret from the McAra was exactly what
Bhaltair had blurted out in Maddock's
earshot.

"No one who belongs to your clan is at our
stronghold, my lord," Althea replied smoothly.
"Master Flen is mistaken."

The old druid must have realized his blun-
der, for he said, "Aye, Laird, at my age I
become easily muddled." He turned to her,
putting on a comical expression of confusion.
"Forgive me, but the lady's name, 'twas
McEvoy, mayhap?"

"I've new blades no' as sharp as you,
Druid." Maddock looked directly at the chieftain. "I shall have the truth of it."

"One of the females stolen with Althea
from her time bears the name Emeline

McAra," Brennus admitted. "From the look of her she's likely of your bloodline. Since kinship isnae the same in the future, and the lady has been afflicted, I thought it best to keep her at Dun Mor."

"You thought it best for a McAra. Yet I'm her laird." His dark brows arched. "I pledged to be your ally, Skaraven. I didnae give you leave to take charge of my blood-kin."

"At best Emeline is only a very distant descendent of yours, my lord," Althea said before her husband could reply. "In our time ladies don't belong to a clan except by name. Most of us leave our families when we become adults and work and live independently, even when we're unmarried."

"I can attest to the truth of that, Laird," Bhaltair put in. "'Tis been my experience."

"You've said enough, Master Flen," Maddock interrupted. "As for your claims, my lady, I've no quarrel with them. But we arenae in your future. You're in my time." Maddock regarded Brennus. "If McAra blood runs in her veins, then this Lady Emeline belongs to my clan. Did she bring with her a husband, Chieftain?"

Brennus's jaw tightened. "No."

The laird nodded. "'Tis then my duty to take charge of an unmarried female of my bloodline. You'll send word to have the lady brought here to me at once."

"I'm no' yours to command, Maddock," he said, sounding almost gentle now. "Ken that I value you and your clan as my closest allies. The Skaraven shall ever be yours. But I cannae give Emeline to you."

Maddock's expression emptied of all emotion. "By keeping my kin from her clan you've released me and mine from our pledge, Chieftain. You're no longer welcome here."

Althea saw Kanyth enter the great hall, followed by several guards, and then jumped as the laird called out to his men to seize the weapons master. Brennus made a subtle gesture, and Kanyth looked perplexed but didn't resist. She knew how easy it would be for her Skaraven men to prevail over the McAra clansmen, and felt a surge of gratitude for her husband's restraint.

"Take him to the dungeons," Maddock ordered. To the druid he said, "Go back to the settlement, Master Flen. We've naught to discuss now."

The old druid glanced at Brennus before he held up his hands in a calming gesture. "This muddle, 'twas my doing. Take me as your hostage, Laird."

"This is really unnecessary," Althea blurted out. "Can't we just sit down and talk about this? There has to be some peaceful compromise we can work out between us."

The laird uttered a sour chuckle. "Small wonder the clans in your time have but shared names." He eyed the old druid. "You've no value here. Get out."

"Do as he says, Bhaltair," Brennus ordered, and watched him trudge out of the stronghold. "Ken that when I leave, Laird, my lady goes with me."

"I dinnae use females as you would," Maddock said, openly sneering now. "Only ken that whatever your purpose in keeping my kin at Dun Mor, it shallnae come without cost."

"I've no purpose but kindness, man." Brennus made a frustrated sound. "She's too ill to make such a journey. Come, I shall take you to Dun Mor, so you may see for yourself."

"Or take me as another hostage?" The laird watched him for a moment. "I'm many things, Chieftain, but no' a fool. 'Tis but two endings to this dispute. You bring my kin to me within threeday, and I shall release yours from my dungeons."

When Althea would have protested her husband simply nodded. "And the other?"

"You prepare for a clan war," Maddock said blandly. "The McAra shall do the same, and we shall enlist other clans we name true allies. This while I find a way to kill your immortal brother."

Chapter Fourteen

❦

IN HER SLEEP Emeline barely moved, which allowed Ruadri to silently savor her beauty. The silken mass of her dark hair had spilled over his chest and neck, and her delicate skin seemed even paler and softer pressed against his flesh. Everything she'd said to him echoed in his thoughts, over and over, like a mind spell he would never break.

You're part of me.

I want to be brave and beautiful for you.

Make me your woman.

Nothing in his training had prepared him for this. He thought he would adore her from afar, in silence, until she returned to her future and the life she'd been born to. Now she lay in his arms, marked by the moon, and made his woman. He had wanted her too much to resist her passionate generosity, but now he realized the enormity of what he had done to her. She had not trifled with any man. She'd saved her maiden night to offer it to him, and he had taken it.

But Emeline was mortal and her life too brief. He had forgotten that but wouldn't again.

Before dawn Ruadri lifted her from his chest, and gently shifted her to his side. She grumbled something and tried to snuggle closer, but he tucked the furs around her before rising and reaching for his trews and tunic. Leaving her in the *broch* was like taking a dagger in his gut, but it could not be helped. She would be safe here among her kin. He would go to warn the Wood Dream alone.

Outside it was as he'd suspected. Ara had posted sentries on the south side of the village to watch for Romans, so he went north before he turned toward the stream. Yet the moment he stepped from the bank into the currents he knew something was wrong.

His body would no longer bond with the water. Trying again and again to transform only resulted in his garments becoming completely soaked. Taking his dagger out, he cut his palm, and immersed it in the stream. When he lifted his hand out of the current, the small wound remained open and bleeding. Seeing the proof that his immortality had been taken from him made Ruadri stagger out of the water.

He had never asked to live forever. Now it seemed he wouldn't, just like Emeline.

Walking until he found a tree-shrouded meadow, Ruadri gathered his thoughts, and then knelt in the center. The cool air still held a trace of the summer wildflowers and lush grasses that carpeted the ground beneath him, reminding him of his lady draped over him. He had never challenged his battle spirit. If he misspoke, the moon might take offense. Now that he had become mortal again, the goddess might also leave him as a dark, wet smear on the pretty spot.

Ruadri found that he didn't care that he had lost eternal life and all its gifts. As for the moon and her fickle nature, for Emeline he would risk anything.

Extending his arms out so that his skinwork caught the moon's soft rays, Ruadri dropped his shadow ward. His body soaked in the thin, silvery light as he offered himself to his battle spirit, and slowly brought together his forearms to complete her symbol.

He looked up at the star-strewn sky. "I beseech you, hear and guide me."

Every sound in the meadow dwindled away as the moon swelled and descended over him, an immense, perfect sphere of pewter-dappled pearl. Although the goddess could take many forms, she always came to him as the shining jewel of the night. This time she blocked out the sky itself with her scope and radiance. When she spoke, he heard her in his heart and his head like the cacophony of thousands of crystal bells ringing.

Do you come to make new demands of me, my warrior, or to beg my forgiveness?

Ruadri started to bow his head as Galan had taught him, but he no longer felt the yoke of servitude that his sire had thrust upon him. Tonight he would find the courage to speak as he would be, as a freed mortal instead of an immortal slave.

"As a lad I offered myself to you, and

yours I remain," he said, looking directly at the sphere. "'Twas no' my choice. He who sired me wished to see me suffer."

Three truths.

"I've another." He extended his cut palm. "I'm made mortal again. I would ask why."

You are mortal in this time.

The portal had given Emeline the ability to understand Ara's language, so the loss of his immortality must have happened for the same reason. He knew the moon to be indifferent to the machinations of druids and their sacred groves. But as much as Ruadri was druid, he was also Pritani. His mother's people had their own magic.

"You marked Emeline McAra. This night again you claimed her, and rode her to speak." He rose to his feet, unwilling to prostrate himself any longer. "She doesnae understand what 'tis meant by your favor. She doesnae belong in this world or mine. I cannae take her as mate."

The moon grew intensely bright, until Ruadri had to shield his eyes with his hand.

You've blinded yourself, son of Fiana. For you chose the soul-sharer. You claimed her innocence and rode her body for your pleasure. You bonded and mated with her. I but gave my consent, and now you both serve me.

"I didnae…"

He stopped as he thought better of it. By Pritani and druid customs he had made Emeline his mate by thought, word and deed. All that remained to do, the ritual blessing, the moon had done herself.

"If she shall be yours as I have been, what would you have of her?"

See to the task before you, Warrior, and all shall be made as will be.

"Ruadri?"

He thought he'd only imagined Emeline's voice, until he turned and saw her standing just at the edge of the moon's nimbus. She had wrapped herself in his tartan, but her bare arms and legs gleamed like new-fallen snow, and her hair hung like a shining blue-black cloak over her shoulders.

Only just remembering to show the proper gratitude, Ruadri knelt and bowed his head. "As you say, so shall be done."

Serve me well, Ruadri Skaraven. That shall be the saving of your lady.

The moon turned into a shower of light that flew up into the sky and ribboned in every direction. Quickly he rose and went to Emeline, who had tipped back her head to watch his battle spirit fade from sight.

"That was the moon," she murmured, her tone filled with awe. "It was hovering over your head." She regarded him with a solemn gaze. "Am I going crazy again?"

"No, lass. 'Twas my battle spirit manifesting for me." He reached for her, and then dropped his hands, unsure if he should touch her just yet. "I summoned her to ask for guidance."

"I heard everything you said, and all of what she told you, in my mind. She sounded like windchimes...or bells." She took a step closer and glanced down at his arms. "We're both glowing."

His skinwork had absorbed the moonlight, as had the scarred crescent on her ankle. Ruadri felt a rush of power and reached for her, only to be hurled backward until he slammed into the ground. He shoved himself upright in time to see a thin silvery spear flying toward him. He jerked up his arms without thinking, and his ink formed the blinding moon.

"Close your eyes," he shouted to Emeline, although he knew it was already too late.

The explosion of power he'd expected never happened. Instead the light spear collided with his skinwork and bent into a V, and then spun away. As he surged to his feet and ran for Emeline, he saw the pointed end of the V hit her abdomen, and then it melted through his tartan and disappeared into her body.

He reached her in time to catch her as she collapsed. "No, no. You shall no' take her from me."

"It's fine," she murmured. Her hair shimmered as she shook her head. "I'm not hurt." She took in a deep breath and pressed her hand over the spot where she had been wounded by the light spear. "It only feels a little strange. Why did you tell me to close my eyes?"

"My power blinds anyone who looks upon it. Until you and now."

Ruadri pushed aside the tartan just as the last glimmer of light faded from her skin. On it now lay another crescent, as dark as his own ink, topped by an inverted, V-shaped rod. In disbelief he traced it with his fingers.

"She marked me again." Emeline peered at the symbols. "Why is it different this time?"

"She's chosen you again," he said, covering the ink before he tucked her head under his chin. "'Tis an ancient sign, the V-rod shielding the crescent. 'Tis the spear bent away from the moon's chosen. By it she names you as my mate, and my protector." The moon must have decided he needed one now that he had become mortal again.

"She chose me to do all that." Emeline sounded bemused. "That's not really necessary."

"'Tis no' by your choice, but my battle spirit doesnae ask." He waited for her to speak in anger, and when she remained silent he drew back to see her expression. She looked completely contented. "Emeline?"

"I don't mind at all. The new ink does match my ankle." She smiled up at him. "Maybe she knows how I feel."

He wished he could. "Emeline, you neednae make light of this."

"I'm not. She knows how I feel about you." She took in a deep breath. "The first moment I saw you, when you came out of the shadows, she poured all her light over you. Maybe that's why I knew I was yours before you even spoke a word to me."

Did he dare believe her? "Why didnae you tell me?"

"I didn't believe it," Emeline admitted. "Then I became so filled with hatred and ugliness and pain that I couldn't think about you anymore. Coming here didn't just heal me. It brought me back to who I was before all this." She pressed her hand over his heart. "This is what I feel for you."

Ruadri felt her power as it swathed him in incandescent joy. She exuded so much of it he pulled her close and fell into her magic and the flowery grasses. In his mind he saw her bliss take form, first as a lush garden filled with bountiful greenery. It grew around them as petals opened and berries swelled. Then came the sound of a soft rain, pattering on a roof above them, and the whispering of a cool breeze through evergreens. He smelled fresh, clean linens and felt the brush of soft yarn sliding through his fingers. Books piled and opened themselves around him, with pages so thin and printing so fine he marveled.

At last a procession of white gowns whirled inside him. The garments had been so finely made and beautifully adorned they seemed worked from spangled clouds. In each one Emeline appeared, her midnight hair braided or curled, laced with ribbons and pearls. One by one the gowns darkened to the amber and black plaid of his tartan and folded themselves around her until she appeared as she was, in his arms.

"I thought it was the dress that mattered," she murmured to him. "It's the woman inside it who has the real beauty."

He wanted to open his heart to her with equal willingness, but the weight of his past betrayal of his clan remained, as onerous and immovable as his guilt. "I've discovered something I must tell you. I've lost my immortality." He showed her the cut on his palm. "Nor can I water-travel."

"I guess we'll walk to the Wood Dream settlement." She gently traced the wound. "Tell me at least you don't mind how I feel about you, or the moon might give me whatever mark that says I'm a weepy wretched stalker of shamans."

Ruadri had never hated himself so much. "I'm no' worthy of your heart, my lady."

"Please, don't say that." Her fingers fluttered over him as if searching for a wound she couldn't see. "Not after what we shared tonight."

"I've never loved," he told her as he captured her hands. "Two Pritani tribes bred the Skaraven to serve as their warrior slaves. My birth killed my mother, and my sire has never forgiven me. Even as I've served the moon, 'twas never from true devotion. But you're too kind and loving to understand what 'tis to have an empty heart."

"I know what it is to be unloved. My parents didn't want children. I was an unhappy accident, and they always resented me for it. I had to take care of them both as they got older, so I never had time for romance. The one friend I had actually didn't care about me." She smiled wanly. "I don't believe you're any more incapable of love than I am. Look at how close you are to your clan."

Now was the time to tell her everything and let her see him as he truly was. To her he was some dream, like the gowns, not the man he had become. Once he revealed himself, however, her feelings for him would be destroyed. For who could love a traitor?

"Shaman?"

Ruadri pulled her up with him and quickly arranged the tartan to cover her body. "We be here, Chieftain."

Ara strode into the clearing, his expression grim. "I feared you be gone already. My allies' watchers sent warning. Many Romans come from the south, hunting *dru-wids*. They shall reach the Wood Dream settlement by mid-morn. I must take the tribe to shelter in the high land."

Ruadri's hands bunched. He'd been a fool to assume they'd have enough time to warn the druids. "Be this the day of solstice?"

"Aye, but 'tis no' time for rituals." Ara gestured back at the village. "Be quick and come with us, and we'll see you kept safe."

Today the Romans would slaughter the Wood Dream, igniting the first flame of the death and destruction spawned by the heartless massacre. Preventing it had to be their task, but the portal had brought them back too late to stop it.

We must reach the settlement before the Romans do.

Never had a task—nor a chance at redemption—ever been made so plain to him.

"My thanks for offer of shelter, but to warn our kind and see them to safety be our duty," Ruadri told Ara. "If you can spare us two quick horses, Chieftain, we shall ride to the sacred stones, and use them to save the Wood Dream."

Chapter Fifteen

✿

LEAVING THE MIDLANDS to return to Dun Mor took Brennus and his wife only a few moments, but it aggravated him even more than being forced to leave his half-brother in the laird's dungeons. A bluster of bitter wind added insult by slapping his face as soon as he released his bond with the river and rode up onto the bank beside Althea. Cadeyrn, who stood with two patrols as if watching for their return, strode down to meet them. Sensing more trouble also waiting, Brennus dismounted, swung his wife down and gestured for the men to come and take the horses.

"The laird discovered we hold the McAra

healer at Dun Mor," he said to Cadeyrn. "He took Kanyth prisoner. He ordered us off his land and prepares for a clan war now. Bring Emeline to me."

"No, Brennus," Althea said before Cadeyrn could reply. "You are not giving Emeline to Maddock."

"'Twill no' be for long. Dinnae glower at me." He regarded his second. "I must seek a truce before the McAra skewer themselves on our swords. For that I need show him the lady afflicted, 'tis all."

"Ruadri and Emeline vanished in the night," Cadeyrn said, stunning him. "The men have checked every level and chamber, but they're nowhere found. Taran and the dark lass took sentries to search the forest for them." He glanced at Althea. "Perrin awaits with Lily in the great hall. She endeavors to bring on a vision of where they go."

"With her head injury? Has she gone crazy, too?" She hurried into the stronghold.

Cadeyrn caught Brennus's arm to prevent him from following. "Kanyth, held prisoner by the little laird? Surely you jest."

"Maddock had him seized and taken to his

dungeons. I couldnae slaughter our mortal allies for that or demanding their blood-kin returned. By mortal reckoning the Skaraven have caused the wrong and must remedy it." He dragged his dripping hair back from his brow. "By the Gods, I go to make peace with the facking druid, and now we face a clan war. Come help me calm our ladies before they declare me their foe."

"We cannae war with the McAra, Bren. 'Twould be like battling bairns." His war master walked with him up to the castle's tor maze and through it entered the great hall. "Manath saw Ruadri last night walking, but alone. None have seen Emeline since the guards took her below. Wherever they went from Dun Mor, they left no tracks."

"Send our hunters to look again." Brennus strode over to Althea, who was sitting beside Perrin with her arm around her. "My ladies, what news?"

The dancer squinted up at him as if in pain. "I have a brand-new headache."

"No visions yet. Take another sip of this, Perr." Lily urged a mug of strong-scented herb brew into her hands before she said to Brennus, "Your shaman was supposed to watch over Emeline. Why would he take her away from us?"

He thought of how angry Ruadri had become when he'd thought Brennus meant to give the healer to Maddock. But his shaman's loyalty to the clan had never once wavered, so he could not believe he would steal away with Emeline.

"I cannae tell you, but we must soon find the lady."

"Maybe we don't have to," Althea said. "We could send word to the McAra that Emeline has gone back to the future."

"Maddock would believe that as much as my claim that she's afflicted." His wife's suggestion put a terrible suspicion in his mind, however. "Cade, did you go out to the sacred grove?"

His second nodded. "'Twas the first place I checked. 'Twere no tracks or sign of them there."

"But would there be, love?" Lily countered. "Maybe Ruadri covered his tracks to make it look as if he hadn't used it."

"Only Emeline may open it," Brennus

reminded her, and then recalled how Lily had first abducted his war master—by clouting him and shoving him into the same portal. "Cade, a word alone."

"Oh, no, you don't." Althea shot to her feet. "Whatever you have to say, say it here. I want all this out in the open."

Had one of his men challenged him so directly, Brennus thought, they would be brawling now. "Wife, 'tis no' the time to question me."

"On the contrary. We should never have left Emeline down in that pit and don't tell me how much you trust your shaman. He's gone. Our friend has a broken ankle, so she didn't magically float out of the fear pit and run away. She also wouldn't go anywhere willingly with Ruadri. She doesn't even like him. You two know something more than you're saying. That's why you want to chat in private." Althea looked from Brennus to Cadeyrn before she planted her hands on her hips. "I'm right, aren't I?"

His war master shrugged. "I've held back naught, my lady."

"Ru had a vision of Emeline before he

awakened to immortality," Brennus finally said. "The same that I did of you, and Cade his lady." As Althea blustered Brennus regarded Lily. "You saw them alone together in her chamber. How did he look upon her?"

"The same way Cade looks at me," Lily said, and sighed. "Completely besotted."

Perrin took a big gulp from the mug. "Well, I don't need a vision now. Ruadri definitely ran off with her. If not through the portal, then on horseback. Even using a cane, Emeline could barely walk."

"Taran accounted for all the mounts," the war master told her.

"I think the Gods despise me." Brennus felt as if the answer were right before him, but he couldn't fathom it. He clamped down on his surging temper and said, "We must find them at once."

"Aye, but until we do we must keep the McAra from declaring war on us," his second said. "When does he expect us to deliver the healer?"

Brennus braced an arm on the mantle and stared down into the hearth's flames. "In threeday."

"We might send a negotiator to ask a full week, and settle for five," Cadeyrn said, and then frowned. "What of Bhaltair Flen?"

"I didnae kill him when he revealed to the laird Emeline being at Dun Mor." Brennus knew what his war master meant, however, and added, "Maddock caught him in more lies and sent him back to the druid settlement near his stronghold. He willnae permit him negotiate for us."

"We may ask," Cade chided. "I shall send messages to the McAra's allies that we seek aid with a truce—"

"Wait a minute," Althea said quickly. "Bhaltair said he had a message from Ruadri about Emeline's affliction. The shaman must have contacted him last night." She thought for a moment. "Could Ru have taken Emeline to the druids so they could treat her?"

"See if Flen sent a reply to Ruadri's message," Brennus ordered Cade, who nodded and rushed off. To his wife he said, "We should change into dry garments."

"Yes, we wouldn't want to catch a chill before the clan war with the McAra." She stalked past him in a huff.

He followed his wife down to their chamber, where she went to the other side of the room to undress. Her back remained stiff, and she said not a word to him as she donned a warm green velvet robe and sat down by the fire to dry her bright copper tresses. He felt her worry as keenly as his own frustration.

"You ken I wouldnae have left Emeline with Maddock."

"I don't know what to think. You keep so many secrets." She glanced up at him. "Like how you knew your shaman was in love with Emeline."

"I but had a notion of it." He ducked to avoid the damp linen she hurled at him. "Very well, I suspected as much. Ru asked that I look for the healer when I found you, and since has spoken fondly of her. Yet Emeline made it plain that she didnae care for him. I thought it a hopeless tangle. I didnae wish to worry you, Wife, so I said naught."

"But now I'm extremely worried, and they're both gone to God knows where. Maddock is furious with us, and we might even have a war on our hands in a few days." Althea combed her fingers through her damp locks as she met his gaze. "I'm a member of this clan. I gave up my life in the future to be with you. Stop treating me like an outsider."

Brennus knelt before her. "Althea, 'tis ever my first thought to protect you, naught else."

"Yes, and I love you for trying." She put her hands on his shoulders. "You and the Skaraven are my family, but so are these women. We need to work together to protect all of them."

He would have kissed her but someone knocked on the door. "Come in and make it quick."

Cadeyrn stepped inside and held out a tiny scroll. "Flen sent this, but no' for Ruadri. 'Tis an invitation for you."

Brennus considered tossing it into the fire, but instead stretched out the strip of parchment and read it. "Flen claims to have something of vital import to the clan. He doesnae name it, but he wishes to meet me at the Aviemore inn to talk of it." He crumpled the scroll. "The tree-knowers have Ruadri and Emeline."

"You don't know that for certain," Althea chided. "Besides, Bhaltair was with us this morning. Why wouldn't he say something about this then?"

"He didnae get his truce," he told her, and eyed his second, who looked just as perplexed as he was. "Never more than now need I your counsel."

"The druids brought us back as immortals to fight the *famhairean*, which we now do," Cadeyrn said. "Of all their kind, Flen has our true measure. He's well aware that taking our shaman and the McAra healer as hostages invites only your wrath. The old man may be called many things, but never that foolish." As Brennus started to speak he held up one hand. "If 'twere anyone else who sent the scroll, would you have the same suspicion of them?"

Sometimes he hated his war master. "No."

"Flen begs to talk," Cade said. "'Twill cost you naught to learn what the old meddler considers of vital import. Mayhap 'tis a measure to mend the rift with the McAra."

"Or more trickery." Brennus glanced at his wife. "I'd have you remain here and see to the search with Cade. No' because I wish to leave you out of the matter."

"I can stay and do that," Althea said, her

expression serene. "See, I trust you not to unleash the wrath of the Skaraven on Bhaltair, no matter what he says, because you don't want to start a war with the druids. Right?"

"Oh, aye. Cade, have a fresh mount saddled and waiting by the river for me." He heard his second cough to cover a laugh and glared at him. "Before I name you Cook and Lily War Master."

Once his second left, his shoulders still shaking, Brennus donned his boots and tartan but armed himself only with two long daggers. He rarely traveled without his sword, but no one could prod his temper like Bhaltair Flen.

Althea walked with him down to the river bank, where she stood on tiptoe to embrace him and press her cheek to his. "I'm sorry I gave you such a hard time. Be safe and come back to me."

He enclosed her in his arms and kissed her until she shivered and sighed against his mouth. "Always, Wife."

Mounting the big tawny mare, Brennus flipped down her blinders before leading her into the icy flows. There he released his physical form to bond with the water, and submerged into a mass of churning, bubbling light. Taking the horse with him, he streamed through the blur of the river and a few moments later surfaced in the loch nearest Aviemore.

As he guided the mare onto the bank she paused to shake her head and flanks before trotting up to the road leading into the tidy rows of cottages and shops. The beginnings of a freezing rain pelted them, and explained the empty thoroughfare as Brennus rode toward the inn. The gnaw of worry over the missing healers receded as the storm grew heavy. He dismounted and took the mare into the village stables, where he rubbed her down with wicking fleeces one of the grooms provided.

"Give her but a fist of oats and a little water," Brennus told the mortal. "I'll no' be long away."

Crossing the main road, he went directly to the inn, and stepped inside. Dozens of candles flickered in the gust of wind from the door, yet no one came to greet him. Despite a large fire burning in the hearth the air smelled oddly stale, as if the place had sat empty for some time. Brennus walked down the hall but saw nothing but lit candles in every room.

"Flen?" he called out, his voice harsh in the stillness. "I've come to talk."

"I'm upstairs, Chieftain" Bhaltair replied from somewhere above his head. "My knee, 'tis badly swollen, and I've broken my walking staff."

Muttering under his breath, Brennus mounted the stairs to go to him. For the first time he noticed that someone had stuffed every window opening with dark cloaks and rugs. A custom among some mortals, he recalled, that meant someone had died in the house. It would explain why the inn stood empty, but why then would the old druid wish to meet here?

On the second floor he saw rooms in two directions, and the last of his patience dissolved. "Flen?"

A door at the far end of one hall swung open. "Here, Chieftain."

Brennus strode toward it, intent on delivering a scalding reproof, and then wood cracked and the floor collapsed beneath his boots. Planks and struts tumbled with him into the kitchen, where he landed on the cold stove with a huge crash. Pots and mugs bounced around him as he rolled off onto his hands and knees, and the warm wetness of his blood streaked down his face. The stink of fish enveloped him as he shook off the debris and then felt pain run him through. He looked down and gritted his teeth as he grabbed a length of broken wood to pull it out of his chest.

From the ugly hole it left behind more blood poured down the front of his tunic and spattered the wet floor. He glanced down to see oil, not rain, soaking the floor and rubble beneath him. Rage and pain suffused him as he stared up at the gaping, ragged hole above him.

"You think to end me, you old fool?" Brennus shouted.

A wooden bucket appeared at the edge of the hole and poured a stream of lamp oil onto his back. The bucket then fell, and he flipped to avoid it crashing into his head. Then he went still as he saw dozens of lit candles floating into the kitchen.

Flen meant to burn him alive.

"Bhaltair, enough," Brennus shouted up to the old druid, who remained out of sight. "I came to talk, naught else."

A high, shrill laugh answered him.

The candles suddenly flew at him from all sides, igniting the lamp oil soaking his tartan. More flames roared up from the debris that had fallen with him, surrounding him on all sides, and the air went black with smoke.

Brennus tore off his burning tartan, spinning around as he looked for a way out.

Through the smoke and flames he spied a door on the opposite end of the room. A wall of fiery debris blocked his path, and he dropped low as he summoned his battle spirit. Vaulting up with a powerful thrust of his legs, he soared over the burning wood, spinning over and over before he crashed into the door. It exploded outward with him, and he fell in a huge pool of half-frozen mud.

Brennus shoved himself to his feet, his tunic and trews smoldering as the rain extinguished his burning garments. Flames now spewed from the inn's upper windows, and black smoke billowed up from the disintegrating roof. He ran around to the front to intercept the old druid, but Bhaltair never showed himself. By then the entire inn blazed.

The groom from the stables rushed over to him. "Master, be you hurt?"

"No." Already the rain had begun to heal his wounds and burns, and wash away the mud, but it did nothing to cool his fury. He watched the roof of the inn collapse into what Bhaltair Flen had planned to make his funeral pyre. "I've been betrayed."

Chapter Sixteen

❧❧❧

R IDING ON THE back of a barely-tamed horse with looped rope reins wearing only a rough blanket made Emeline actually miss the fourteenth century. As she tried to keep her seat on the furiously galloping beast, she decided never again to complain about the bulky wooden saddles or primitive leather tack the medieval riders used. At least Ruadri stayed close to her side, so that if she fell off he'd probably be able to grab her.

When I fall off.

Emeline began slipping back, and gripped the horse's sides tighter with her legs. In that moment her body adjusted to the animal's movements, and a strange confidence filled her. Riding was familiar now, in the same way understanding the tribe's language was.

The ground rushed under her in a threshing blur as they reached the clearing with the circle of carved stones, and she could finally tug the horse to a halt. Ruadri swung off his mount and reached for her, hoisting her off and down onto the ground.

"What if the portal sends us back in time again?" she asked as they hurried over to the stones. "I don't want to end up somewhere being chased by dinosaurs."

"We must have faith," the shaman said, gripping her hand as they stepped inside the circle. "The Gods brought us here to save the Wood Dream. They wouldnae thwart us now."

Emeline took in a deep breath before she crouched down and placed her hand in the center of the circle. The grass was cool and wet from morning dew, but the ground remained solid. She closed her eyes and envisioned the whirling vortex that should have opened. When she looked again the portal remained closed. Emeline took away her hand, tried again, and then slowly straightened.

"Your Gods are not cooperating."

Ruadri made an impatient sound, and knelt down to place his hand over the mark hers had left in the grass. A furious hail of small burning stones blazed inside Emeline as she felt the intensity of his anger and frustration, but what confused her was his attempt to open the portal.

"You can't do that," she reminded him. "Unless you know some kind of spell–"

"I've opened many portals." He bowed his head, and then looked at her, his eyes so dark they looked almost black. "I'm half-druid."

Emeline felt as if he'd knocked her sideways. "But you told me two Pritani tribes bred the Skaraven."

"Aye, and so they did—all except me." He drew back his hand, and then struck the ground with his fist. "By the Gods, we come to do your will. *Open so we may.*"

His bellowed words echoed around the clearing, and seemed to shake the oak branches, but the ground remained intact.

Ruadri opened his fist and regarded the unhealed cut across his palm.

"They've taken all from me."

"No. You've still got me." Emeline urged him to his feet. His bleak expression made her reach for his hands. The moment she touched him she felt as if she were sinking into black quicksand—sensing his emotions—but she wouldn't let go, not now. "I don't understand. What did the druids do to you?"

"My sire, Galan, was druid kind." He looked over her head at the oaks before he met her gaze. "He and Bhaltair Flen secretly bred and trained me to serve as their watcher—to spy on my brothers and tell them all that they did. I'm no' only half-druid, my lady. I'm a traitor."

No wonder she felt as if she might drown from the inside out. His guilt and shame spread inside her as huge and encompassing as a swamp of darkness. Yet as overwhelming as his emotions were, she sensed nothing evil in the dreadful torrents—just the opposite.

"Does anyone in the clan know about this?" When he shook his head, Emeline felt the yellow grit of his self-disgust ricochet inside her. "Did they also make you keep it secret from Brennus and the others?"

"In my boyhood Galan swore he would poison them all if I refused to spy. I didnae dare risk that." He met her gaze. "When I grew to a man, I thought of killing him. But I couldnae do it. I dinnae ken why."

"He was your father," Emeline said.

Ruadri's mouth flattened. "No. Galan but sired me. After my mother died, he tortured me and called it training. He made me offer myself to the moon. He plagued every moment of my life, as he does still. But father, no. Never could he be."

"That doesn't stop you from being his son," she said softly.

"Could I pry every part of Galan from me, I would," Ruadri assured her.

A terrible pity filled her. He had obviously carried these feelings since childhood, hiding them deep inside his heart. The burden of that weighed so heavily on her, and she'd felt them only for a few moments. How could he have endured them alone for so long?

Emeline knew what she had to do, and held onto his hands when he would have released her.

She knew nothing that she said would take away his torment, so she focused on giving herself to him. Into him she sent the sparkling champagne of her delight in finding him, fountaining from her thoughts to his in a gilded, bubbling froth. With the rich red velvet of the longing she'd felt for his touch she stroked through him, veiling it with the midnight silk lace of her deepest desires. From her memories of their glorious night together she fed him confections of the delicious pleasures he'd shown her.

The more she gave him, the paler his darkness grew. Blue diamonds of her faith in him set themselves in the golden crown of her adoration, which she offered him without hesitation. She wrapped all of her feelings for him in the snowy white gown of the innocence she'd given him, and made herself the bride of his heart.

"You'll never be alone again," Emeline said as she watched her emotions glowing in his wet eyes. "What you were or are or will be doesn't matter, as long as we're together. You have me now."

The shaman swept her up in a fierce

embrace, his hands stroking over her hair and back as the last of his bleak emotions dwindled away. In their place sprouted the beginnings of a garden, with pale shoots of hope so lovely and fragile they made her swallow a sob.

Ruadri set her at arm's length. "'Tis more I must tell you, but soon 'twill be too late to save the Wood Dream. We must go to the settlement before the Romans reach it."

Emeline hurried back with him to their horses. This time she hoisted herself onto her mount using a fallen tree trunk, and without thinking took up the reins as Ruadri held his. Wheeling the horse toward the trail, she glanced at her lover.

"I'll follow you."

The shaman nodded and urged the big horse into a quick trot.

Keeping pace with Ruadri also proved easy for Emeline, and once they cleared the forest they raced around the village and down a grassy stretch parallel to the stream. The sun and wind burnished her face, and her hair whipped into a tousled tangle. Still she kept up, as confident as if she'd been born in the saddle.

Maybe I was reborn in it when we came here.

The shaman suddenly reined in his mount to a stop at the edge of a broad glen hemmed by incredibly huge, gnarled oaks and colossal pines. Quickly she tugged on the reins to do the same and followed the direction of his gaze. A cloud of what looked like yellow smoke rose into the sky beyond the ancient forest.

"'Tis dust from the cart road, stirred by foot soldiers," Ruadri said, his jaw tightening. "Only Romans could raise so much."

"Which direction is the settlement?" Emeline asked, and turned her head as he pointed to a narrower trail leading east. "How far away?"

"Three leagues, mayhap four." He gave the dust cloud another hard look before he said, "I shall divert them. You ride ahead and warn the tribe."

"While they cut you to pieces? You're mortal now, remember?" Emeline reached over to grab his reins with her free hand. "We have to do this together. So, you come with me, or I go with you."

"Then together to the Wood Dream." Ruadri leaned over to kiss her, and took back the reins. "Ride as fast as you may, my lady."

She turned toward the settlement and moved forward before she used the pressure of her legs to bring the horse to a canter. Soon she and the shaman were galloping across the glen for the oaks. But as they sped past the lake, Emeline spotted something odd. Two people stood in the shallows, doing what Emeline could only call frolicking—while the Romans attacked up ahead. But her astonishment turned to shock when she finally recognized them: Hendry and Murdina.

"There they are," Ruadri shouted.

But when she turned to him, he wasn't pointing at the two druids. Up ahead what looked like giant, thick-bodied warriors stood in a long line. As they drew closer she saw that they were enormous carvings sculpted from massive trees still rooted in the ground, and their faces matched that of the *famhairean*.

A rusty claw of savage emotion raked through her, as she looked over to see the vanguard of the Roman army entering the glen. At the front, mounted officers wearing gray armor and helmets flanked tight formations of marching soldiers carrying rectangular shields, short, wide-bladed swords, and long spears with iron heads. Their faces looked almost impassive, but the hideous emotions seething under those blank expressions made bile surge up from her belly.

A sharp whistle came just before something flew past her cheek, and Ruadri vaulted off his horse to knock her to the ground. Men shouted as he hauled her up and carried her into the forest. As one of the trees sprouted an arrow she finally understood: someone was shooting at them.

Ruadri pushed her behind one of the huge totems, and shielded her with his body as leaves crunched beneath heavy footsteps coming at them.

"You've fine mounts, heathen," a flinty voice called out. "What of that dark little mare you hide from us? Will she hold two riders?"

The Roman's putrid lust nearly melted down Emeline's mental block before the shaman's strength swept it away like a silvery tide beneath a full moon.

"Close your eyes now, my lady," Ruadri murmured. "Dinnae open them again until I return."

She knew he said that his power blinded, but he was asking too much of her. How could she just stand here alone and do nothing? Her side and ankle grew hot, and her terror receded as a calm, glowing power coursed through her. It seemed she wouldn't be alone.

"Come back to me."

As Ruadri kissed her brow and left her there the serenity of his battle spirit filled her heart, soothing her frantic emotions. It spread from there, gently reinforcing the crumbling blockade in her mind until it grew into a gleaming fortress of moonlight. It quieted her fear as she heard the crude taunts of the Romans, and then their hoarse screams and stumbling movements. All around her the trees rustled, although there was no wind now, and then she felt an azure wash of wrenching sorrow. It came from Ruadri, not the men he'd just blinded. Despite the tranquil presence of the moon in her mind Emeline was furious.

How could you curse him with such a terrible power?

Indeed, I have favored the son of Fiana, the voice of a thousand bells ringing whispered from inside her head. *To serve me, a warrior must suffer my power as well as wield it. Few have proven brave enough to do both, as well you know by the soul-sharing granted you, daughter of Seonag.*

Emeline refused to cringe as the power inside her made her scars burn as if she were being branded.

Neither of us ever asked for your favors.

Nor I yours, Emeline. Your task yet awaits. See to it, else you lose all that you love.

"Emeline." Ruadri was shaking her. "Gods, look at me."

Slowly she opened her eyes and felt a final cool stream of power as the battle spirit faded from her thoughts.

"I just insulted the moon, I think." She blinked a few times, and then saw the blood spattering the side of his face. "Oh, God, you're hurt."

"No, lass. 'Tis their blood." He caught her before she stepped away from the totem. "The horses have run off, and the Romans have crossed the glen."

"We can't give up." She hurried out and stumbled to avoid the two bodies locked together on the ground. The Romans had thrust their swords in each other, their blinded eyes staring up at the sky. "Your power did that to them?"

"I took their sight." Ruadri sounded indifferent, but his mouth tightened as he regarded the dead men. "They thought each other me."

Emeline gripped his hand. "Come on. I have it on good authority that our task yet awaits. We'll make it. We have to."

Running through a forest beside the big shaman seemed another impossible undertaking. In her time Emeline had always struggled with moving quickly. Her curves tended to joggle when she did, and she grew quickly out of breath. When she hurried to a patient's room it always made the other nurses snicker. Now she didn't care what bounced or bobbled, not when so many lives were at stake. Thanks to starvation she was much lighter on her feet, and she seemed to be much more sure-footed than she'd ever been in her life.

Within a few minutes they reached the edge of the settlement, where they stopped and looked around at the well-tended gardens and tidy little cottages. The Wood Dream took good care of their settlement, which now stood empty.

The druids had vanished.

Chapter Seventeen

RETURNING TO THE Sky Thatch settlement took longer than Bhaltair would have wished, but his pony began to limp a league from the McAra stronghold. Unwilling to ride a lame mount, he instead walked while leading the beast at a slow pace. High overhead, the sun barely made itself felt, and the cold air rifled through his robes like darts of ice

"I would go to Dun Mor to beg forgiveness of Brennus, you ken," he told the pony as they made their way through the snow-covered grain fields. "Only he'd slay me before I uttered a word."

His mount arched his neck, drawing Bhaltair's gaze to the evergreens ahead of them, where he could see Fingal on horseback, speaking to his defenders. The headman must have spotted him, for he rode out to intercept him.

"You've saved me a long, hard ride to McAra's castle," the headman said as he nimbly leapt down from his saddle. "Cora went an hour ago to wake Oriana and found her bed empty. I searched the entire settlement, but she's gone."

Bhaltair rubbed his brow. "Gone to where?"

"We dinnae ken, but she didnae cross our boundary wards, so I imagine she used our sacred grove." Fingal hesitated before he said, "More I must show you at the cottage."

The headman accompanied him to the settlement, where Cora stood waiting outside their home. She looked pale and tired but forced a smile as she greeted Bhaltair.

"At first I thought Oriana left us to join you," Cora said as she accompanied them inside. "Fingal went to check her room for a note, and…well, you look cold. I shall make a warming brew." She hurried off to the kitchen.

Bhaltair had never seen the druidess so flustered. "What has the lass done now?"

"Much you didnae ken, I think," his old friend said, nodding at their dining table. On it sat Oriana's open satchel, a bundle of garments, a comb and a pair of slippers.

He went over to examine the possessions. "You took out her things? Why?"

"I noticed a small bulge in the bed and found the bag stuffed beneath the ticking. When I pulled it out it felt over-heavy," Fingal explained as he went over to the table. "I left the cause of it that I found inside, beneath the false bottom." He reached in, removed a panel of leather, and gestured for the older druid to look for himself.

Suddenly Bhaltair didn't want to see what it was, and sat down heavily. "She's young, Fin, and so distressed over Gwyn's murder by the *famhairean*. I've done almost naught to train her while demanding too much work. Whatever she's hid, 'tis my fault."

"I think no'," the headman said, and took out a long, double-edged ritual dagger, placing it gently before him. Then he produced a large vial half-filled with a murky liquid and uncorked it before setting it beside the blade.

Neither should have been in Oriana's possession.

"Your acolyte carries a ritual killing blade," Fingal said softly. "The like I've no' seen for many centuries."

"Gods," Bhaltair breathed as he stared at the archaic weapon, which had a curved, patinated hilt covered in protective glyphs. Among them had been carved tiny crescents layered together like the scales of a serpent. The pounding ache in his knee and the sorrow clenching his heart intensified as he picked up the blade. His hand grew stiff and cold as the death that clung to it touched his flesh. "This belonged to Barra Omey."

Fingal drew back from him. "Barra the bone-conjurer? How? She fled Scotland more than fifty years past."

"Aye, 'twas that or face the conclave." He put down the dagger and rubbed his throbbing hand. "'Twas this very dagger she used for her ritual sacrifices. I've read the archive scrolls on her ruling. She always carried it with her."

"Then how could Oriana have it?" the headman asked, looking perplexed now.

"Someone makes evil use of the lass." Cora brought a steaming cup to Bhaltair, and used a linen to pick up the dagger and vial and put both back inside the satchel. "Take this away, Husband. I'll no' have that murderess's belongings poisoning our home."

"I'll set it by the woodpile." Fingal stuffed the rest of Oriana's possessions into the satchel and carried it outside.

Cora sat down across from Bhaltair. "My husband had gone to the well long before the conclave ruled against Barra. But I became an acolyte the same year she fled justice. The herbalist who trained me spoke much on the evils she did. She sought to resurrect those she killed with that blade." She gave him a direct look. "Could your lass be her daughter?"

"'Tis unlikely. Barra never mated. If she did after she vanished, she would have been my age at the time of Oriana's birth." Bhaltair took a sip of the spicy cannel brew and warmed his hands on the sides of the cup. "Mayhap the lass found the dagger by chance. She wouldnae ken what it was."

"Aye. 'Twas likely sitting in a meadow somewhere, just beside a vial of the most powerful sleeping potion concocted by druid kind." Cora reached to touch his trembling hand. "I've seen that you have much affection for the lass. But we've proof now that she's drugged you, and from what Fingal has said, often. She carries a killing blade. If she meant to end a master like you, Bhaltair, the only manner in which she could would be while you slept."

He met her concerned gaze. "If 'tis true, then why do I yet breathe? And why would she leave behind her satchel?"

"I reckon she meant to return in secret and have us believe she never left," Fingal said, joining them. "I put defenders around the portal when we found the lass missing. One of them came to say they just saw her emerge from it."

"I must speak with her at once." Bhaltair shoved his chair back and stood. "Where do you have her?"

"As soon as she spied our men she leapt back inside." The headman caught his arm as he hobbled toward the door. "You cannae try to follow her."

"I dinnae fear an untrained speak-seer who pretends herself a bone-conjurer," Bhaltair snapped. "What shall she do when I confront her? Invite Gwyn to scold me?"

"You dinnae ken who Oriana may have channeled," Cora countered. "'Twouldnae be difficult for a druidess as powerful as Barra to persuade the lass to do her bidding."

"But why then plot against me? I didnae serve on the conclave when they ruled against Barra," Bhaltair said slowly. "I spent that spring in the west, training gifted ovates from three tribes in the crystal arts. By the time I journeyed back she had already fled. 'Twas all done without me."

"Did your path ever cross Barra's?" Fingal asked.

What Bhaltair knew of the bone-conjurer had come from the conclave's archives, and grim recounting of the circumstances by some of his friends among the ruling elders. According to them Barra had despised tribal life, and had gone into seclusion as soon as she completed her training. That solitude allowed her to practice her blood rituals in secret for many years before she had been exposed.

Now that he thought on it, if she wished to be alone, then why did she keep trying to resurrect her victims?

Such abhorrence of druid life seemed completely alien to him, much like Oriana's intractable hatred of the Skaraven, whom she blamed for Gwyn's death. Since he had failed to convince them upon awakening to challenge the *famhairean*, perhaps she held him responsible, too.

He looked up at Fingal. "I shallnae pursue her alone, but we must find her."

A horn blew an alarm outside the cottage, and Fingal went to sweep aside the window covering and look out. His expression turned grim. "Cora, go and help gather the young and old, and take them to the portal. Bhaltair, with me."

His wife embraced him quickly before she hurried away.

Bhaltair followed the headman out of the cottage to see the tribesmen arming themselves with scythes. Only the most serious threat to the settlement would compel every druid to take up their blades.

"Do the *famhairean* attack?"

"Someone does," his friend replied, his young features darkening.

A pale-faced ovate trotted up and handed a scythe to Fingal. "The defenders warn that many mounted warriors approach, Master Tullach. They bear blades ready, but they dinnae wear the McAra tartan. They wear many, and all different."

Bhaltair shook his head as another druid offered him a scythe. "I shallnae need it, lad."

He accompanied Fingal and the armed tribesmen out of the settlement and into the evergreens bordering their boundary. There they stood in the shadows and watched as a large group of immense warriors with swords drawn rode toward them. Bhaltair recognized the ancient attack formation as well as the many, different-colored tartans worn by the clansmen.

"'Tis the Skaraven," he told his friend. Had Brennus felt it necessary to bring with him a warband simply to end him? Bhaltair was almost flattered. "They've no grievance with the Sky Thatch, so they come for me."

Fingal tried to stop him, but he tugged free and limped out to meet the chieftain, who as always rode at the front of his clan. Bhaltair halted when Brennus drew close enough for him to see his wet, scorched garments, and the dark fury of his expression. Something terrible had obviously happened to the chieftain, and it seemed the blame had been put on his head.

Bhaltair could cast a spell with enough power to knock the chieftain off his saddle and fling him across the fields, but knew of none to defeat a warband of immortals. Since his actions might result in harm to the Sky Thatch, he elected to tuck his hands in his sleeves and wait to be attacked.

A spear buried itself in the ground next to his boot, the shaft quivering as if impatient to be hurled again. The clan shifted their mounts so that they presented a narrower target while readying for a charge. Behind him Bhaltair could feel the Sky Thatch preparing as well. The air grew thick with unseen waves of leashed brute force and summoned magic— and he in the very center of it all.

This had not been caused by the rift between the Skaraven and the McAra.

The chieftain hoisted himself up, flipped over his stallion's head and landed before Bhaltair, yanking the spear from the earth. "Your trap failed."

Now Bhaltair saw the blood rimming the jagged tear in Brennus's tunic, and traces of the same on his face, but held onto his composure.

"I dinnae ken your meaning, Chieftain."

"I escaped before the flames consumed the inn." He brought up his sword and poised its honed tip a whisper away from Bhaltair's neck. "'Tis the final time you work your trickery on me."

A fire at an inn…that likely was the inn at Aviemore, where he'd often met with Ruadri. He knew it to be shuttered since the sudden death of the innkeeper's wife.

"I set no trap for you, lad," Bhaltair said, and felt pain and a warm trickle run down his neck. "I worked no trickery. You've been deceived."

The sharp cry of a raven shattered the air

as blue light glowed beneath the chieftain's tunic.

"*Dinnae lie to me again.*"

"I came directly here from the McAra's castle, walking beside my lame mount," Bhaltair said, and lifted his chin. If the man wished to end him, he would not resist. "I've gone nowhere else."

For a moment he thought the furious chieftain might ignore his words and take his head anyway, and then Brennus bellowed, "War Master, counsel."

Cadeyrn's streaked hair whipped away from his stern face as he came to stand beside them. "Tell me all that you have done since leaving the McAra this morn." The war master watched without blinking as Bhaltair repeated his story for him, and then said to Brennus, "I see no sign of deception." He leaned forward and drew in a deep breath. "His robes smell clean, and he hasnae smoke or singe marks on him."

"More trickery," Brennus insisted. "He called out to me, thrice."

"But you told me that you didnae see him once, and a voice may be aped." The war master's shrewd gaze shifted to the druids standing ready before he regarded Bhaltair again. "Flen could go anywhere to escape our vengeance. Why return to this settlement, where we knew him to be? When the defenders sighted us, why did he remain, and come to meet us? I stand with you, Chieftain, but I believe him."

For a moment Brennus's arm bulged with knotting muscle, and then the chieftain slowly lowered his sword. "Then 'twas treachery meant to end us both," he said, his tone gruff.

"'Twould seem that," Bhaltair said, feeling the flush of relief a moment before the cold sweat of dread inched down his spine.

For he now knew where Oriana had gone this morning: to Aviemore, to kill the Chieftain of the Skaraven.

Chapter Eighteen

SEEING THE EMPTY settlement left Ruadri feeling so bitter that he might as well have been chewing on spotted thistle. The only reason the entire tribe would have left their homes would be to gather for their solstice ritual in the glen. He sensed it had already begun. He could feel the celebratory magic spreading out around them. The powerful spell would never be completed. In a few moments the Romans would pour into the glen to attack and slaughter them.

Like the dwindling smoke rising from the cottage chimneys, all their efforts to warn the Wood Dream had been wasted.

"I don't understand." Emeline turned around slowly, peering at the vacant cottages.

"Everything pointed to this being why we were brought here. We were supposed to save them."

For the first time Ruadri wondered if that were true. They had completely failed, yet nothing that had happened since they'd arrived in this time had helped them. It almost seemed as if the Gods had meant to keep them from preventing the massacre.

Emeline faced him. "How far away is the place where they're holding the ritual?"

"Too far," he said tonelessly. "We cannae reach it on foot before the Romans do."

She reached for the base of her throat, and then dropped her hand. "We have to do something."

Did they? Slowly his hands knotted at his sides. He didn't care that he had been made mortal again, or that he might be trapped in this time for good. He'd been born to both. The miseries inflicted on him he saw as his due, for the very first act of his existence had been to kill his own mother. But he had risked Emeline's life to come here and save the Wood Dream. Emeline, who had been brutalized and afflicted by the mad druids. Who put her faith in him even knowing him a traitor. Who had urged him on when he would have given up.

Emeline, who deserved none of this.

Ruadri felt rage unlike any he'd ever known seeping into the hollowness inside him. With this cruel ruse the Gods had finally asked too much of him.

"Look," Emeline said, tugging on his hand and pointing toward a vegetable garden. "Our horses have come back. We can ride to the glen."

He went with her to catch the grazing mounts, but stopped her from climbing onto her saddle. "I shall go and do what I may. You must wait here for me." When she started to protest he took hold of her shoulders. "Hundreds of peaceful folk shall die there by the blade. Do you no' ken how it will be, to feel their horror and pain?"

"I'm stronger now, I can…" She suddenly choked and doubled over, clutching at her abdomen.

"'Tis begun." Ruadri held onto her and turned his head toward the distant sound of screaming. The skinwork on his forearms

turned white and burned like flaming ice. He
had never wished to kill, and that, too, had
been taken from him. "I must see to the
Romans. I'll return for you when 'tis done."

Keeping her away from the massacre was
the only kindness he could offer her. As Ruadri
mounted his horse and rode for the glen, a
strange peace settled over him. In his boyhood
Galan had always derided him for avoiding
violence and refusing to inflict harm. He'd had
to threaten him with death to force him to
fight as a warrior as well as a druid. He'd
thought him weak and heartless, and entirely
unworthy to bear the name Skaraven.

Ruadri would at last do his evil sire proud.

The sounds of killing and terror grew
louder as he rode through the forest to the
glen. He caught glimpses of young druids
running toward their settlement, chased by
Romans with bloody swords. Every tree he
passed had gone still, as if turned to stone. A
strangeness in the air bit at him like a swarm
of tiny, vicious insects, and birds began dropping from the sky. At the rim of the trees the
surface of the tribe's loch went as flat as ice,

soon pocked by the bobbing bodies of dead fish.

A wet, rusted iron smell filled his lungs as the stench of death came to greet him.

His blazing forearms lost their heat as Emeline and her mount appeared beside him. Tears streamed down her white face, and she shook so much he thought she might fall to the ground. Ahead he saw the Romans and druids in the glen, and reached for her reins to stop both horses.

"You cannae go any nearer," he told her flatly. "'Twill be too much for you to bear." When he began to dismount she lunged at him, knocking them both to the ground.

"Neither can you," she said, sobbing the words into his chest. "Please, listen to me. It's the giants. They're coming alive. They're coming for the Romans. *Ruadri.*"

The ground beneath them trembled, and behind them trees fell by the dozens. Something massive was coming toward them from the settlement, something that stood nearly as tall as the very tops of the oldest oaks. Ruadri sensed dangerous enchantment spreading out in a shadowy cloud all around the movement, and Emeline released a terrible cry.

A wooden giant smashed into view, its carved features splintering as it opened a cart-size maw. The roar that came from the totem's gaping mouth stripped the leaves from every branch around it in a flurry of tattered green. It swatted aside a massive oak, stepping over the quivering roots with the huge blocks that served as its feet. Ruadri rolled with Emeline to avoid being crushed, and then gathered her up and ran out of the path of the other giants that followed.

He saw the grove of trees heavily draped with golden mistletoe, where the Wood Dream had fashioned an altar of rubbed oak. There he ran to take shelter under the vines.

"God in heaven," Emeline whispered.

Gleaming berries pelted them as the living totems burst into the glen. The Romans froze and gaped at the giants advancing on them. One of the mounted soldiers shouted and recklessly charged at them. A huge hand slammed down upon them to crush both man and horse together. When the horrific mangle fell to the ground it sent the blood-soaked attackers scattering in every direction.

Ruadri had killed many Romans, but that had been on the battlefield, against armed men intending to end him. Here was nothing but pure butchery.

"I saw Hendry and Murdina swimming in the loch when I rode past it," Emeline told him in a shaking voice. "They were splashing each other like children. They're not doing this."

Everyone had assumed that the *famhairean* had been brought to life by the mad druids, but the towering totems had done so on their own. Ruadri realized that the Wood Dream had not simply carved warrior statues to frighten away invaders. They had imbued them with magic to defend the settlement against attack.

The mistletoe vines around them began to wither and blacken, and Emeline gasped as the sunlight faded. Ruadri tried to reach for her, and found he couldn't move. His skinwork took on its battle glow, and the same dark light radiated from his lady's side and ankle. The deep blue radiance reached their faces, masking them before it funneled into their eyes

"You and your lady must see," Emeline said, her voice taking on the bell-like resonance of his battle spirit. "Look upon the dead."

Through the dark light he watched glorious, incandescent shimmers rising from the lifeless bodies of the Wood Dream. Although he should not have been able to see them, he knew them to be the souls of the druids. As with all druids, the death of their bodies would return them to the well of stars to await rebirth.

Yet as the giants stalked after the retreating Romans, the soul-lights stopped rising, as if trapped in the glen by some unseen force. When the totems drew close tendrils of yellow light snaked out from their wooden bodies and wrapped around the tribe's souls, dragging them to the giants. They sank inside the huge bodies and disappeared.

Ruadri kept fighting the power holding him in its grip, and Emeline turned to face him. In her eyes he saw the moon eclipse the lovely blue of her irises, and then knew this was his battle spirit's doing. They had been made to come here, but not to save —to watch.

"I dinnae ken how this can be," he told her. "How can they steal the souls of druids?"

"The Wood Dream enchanted their totems to protect the tribe." As the moon spoke through her, Emeline trembled and swayed. "The druids didnae understand their nature. To the giants 'tis no difference between flesh and spirit."

Once they absorbed the last of the trapped souls, the giants went still as the carved statues they had once been. Ruadri saw their forms changing, as if swallowing the tribes' souls had sparked the transformation. Their faces smoothed, and their limbs and torsos became refined with joints and muscles. Their heads darkened where human hair would have grown. Even their blocky hands and feet became articulated and sprouted fingers and toes. It chilled him when they finished, and yet looked nothing like the slender, ethereal-looking druids that had enchanted them.

The totems had modeled their new forms

after the Romans as they developed into
famhairean.

The surviving soldiers uttered furious
shouts and attacked their colossal twins,
hacking at the unmoving totems with their
swords. When they managed to fell one, they
swarmed over it and used their axes to split its
face in half. The injured totem let out a shrill,
creaking sound that roused the others from
their trance. Moving much faster now, they
seized the soldiers and dragged them away
from the wounded *famhair*, and hefted their
writhing bodies high above them.

"I beg you, protect my lady," Ruadri said,
knowing what the giants meant to do as they
opened their huge mouths. "She cannae with-
stand what comes."

"Can you, Warrior?" Emeline asked, and
then abruptly crumpled at his feet.

The Romans who realized their fate
struggled and shouted, frantically trying to
escape the giants' hands. The bulge-eyed
terror on their faces made Ruadri almost feel
sorry for them. Romans had always been the
most brutal and feared of warriors, but no
more. One by one they dropped into the

cavernous maws as the *famhairean* ate them alive.

Ruadri silently offered thanks to the moon for sparing his lady, and when the last soldier had been devoured, the dark light finally dispersed. He dropped to his knees, turning Emeline onto her back. The bed of moss surrounding the altar had cushioned her fall, and the only marks he found on her had been left by her tears.

"*Caraidean.*"

Ruadri lifted Emeline against his chest as he stood and looked toward the sound of the shout. A young druid in wet, flapping robes chased after a naked druidess rushing toward the giants. The lass halted when she saw the dead littering the glen, and then clutched the sides of her head and tore at her hair as she screamed. The druid caught her hands and pulled her against his chest as he wrapped her in a dark woolen cloak.

Ruadri recognized them at once: Hendry Greum and Murdina Stroud.

Slowly the *famhairean* came to surround the pair, forming a large circle. Hendry said something in a voice too low for Ruadri to hear over Murdina's sobs, and the giants shuffled closer. Whatever the druid murmured next to them, it dispelled the savagery distorting their expressions. Their mouths and chests still dripping with Roman blood, the giants knelt down and bowed their massive heads.

They devour the Romans alive, and from this day forth shall harm every druid or mortal to cross their path, Ruadri thought. *Yet they pay homage to these two.*

Unable to fathom why, he turned his back on the scene and carried Emeline away from the glen.

Chapter Nineteen

✤✤✤

E MELINE WALKED THROUGH the blackest night, her bare feet stirring up ash-colored dust. The cratered wasteland around here seemed very familiar, and yet completely alien. It looked like a cold place, but her skin was hot, as if she'd been badly sunburned. Curving out around her, the sky held millions of glittering stars, but no moon. She vaguely remembered being in a different place and watching terrible things. Things that had tried to…but she didn't want to think about that. That was finished, all finished.

Like her. She was absolutely done with everything but walking.

"Em, where have you been?" Meribeth

Campbell said as she appeared in her path. Resplendent in her sequined ivory wedding gown, she used a thin hand to brush her long, lace-edged veil back from her perfectly made-up face. "And what are you wearing?"

Emeline glanced down to see she wore nothing but an amber and black tartan wrapped like a sarong. As cold as the waste-land was, she should have dressed warmer. Then again, she was so heated now she didn't need it.

"Well?" Meri demanded.

"I've been away." A memory of a huge man with intense gray eyes flashed through Emeline's mind, and she walked past the other woman. "What are you doing here?"

"I don't know. I was just retaking pictures. Of course, the photographer botched half of them, the bloody fool." Meri fell into step beside her, lifting eight yards of satin skirt to reveal satin slippers edged with pearls. "You missed my wedding, you know. Lauren had to take your place at the last minute."

Emeline chuckled and shook her head. "I'll bet you didn't have to whidder her to it."

"I wish I hadn't. She got drunk at the

reception and grabbed my husband's crotch. Can you believe she demanded he show her the size of his banger? He's still a little sore." Meri wrinkled her nose. "Anyway, I'm never speaking to her again."

"I'm sorry." Though Emeline wasn't, it seemed the thing to say.

Her friend waved her hand. "Not that Jared shouldn't suffer a little. He booked us in the cheapest resort he could find. Stained sheets, a green pool, and no room service. On my honeymoon! Then I let him talk me into going for a dip in the ocean."

As her best friend described what a swarm of sea lice had done to her, Emeline absently stroked the soft wool of the tartan. It made her feel better to touch it. But who had given it to her? Not Meri, who was allergic to wool.

"…so, I told Jared, no monkey business until the rash healed, because I had it everywhere. What does he do? Went off on me, right there in the hotel's lousy restaurant. I've never been more mortified." Her friend glared at her. "Why don't you say something? Em, are you even listening to me?"

Emeline nodded. "Your new husband is a

cheapskate and has bruises on his boabie. Lauren is still Lauren. You had a miserable honeymoon with painful dermatitis and no sex. It's exactly as it should have been."

"What are you blethering?" Meribeth tugged her to a stop. "This was supposed to be the happiest time of my life."

"Was it?" Perhaps it was time for her former best friend to face the consequences of her actions. "To find real happiness you have to love someone. You have to give instead of take. You have to think about them as much or more than yourself."

"I do," her friend screeched.

"You married Jared because he was a rich doctor. Now you know why he has so much money: he doesn't like to spend it. We all know Lauren drinks too much around you, because later she can blame the whiskey for what she says and does." Emeline saw Meri's gaping expression and sighed. "You should divorce Jared and make up with Lauren. She's in love with you, and you'll probably be happier with her."

Her best friend gave her a measuring look

and sniffed. "I liked you better when you were fat. You were much sweeter."

Emeline didn't feel alarmed as Meribeth began to fade away. "You never liked me."

Once again alone in the wasteland, Emeline buried her face in the tartan, and breathed in the scent of the gray-eyed man. He hadn't said he loved her, but she knew he wanted her, and cared about her. She wanted to be with him, but he wasn't here. He'd stayed behind in that place where the horrible things had happened.

"You have to go back, too, honey."

Emeline watched as Althea Jarden climbed out of a crater, her green silk medieval gown covered in dust. Her lovely copper-red hair had turned silver-white, as had her eyes, skin and everything but the dress.

"Althea. You look like a goddess."

"I should. I am a goddess," her friend said as she shook out her skirt, sending a billowing cloud around them.

Emeline squinted at her. "You're the moon."

"Yep. At first, I thought sending along that nurse friend of yours would help. What a selfish little twit she is." Althea smiled. "Any-way, I've manifested as your American friend because you actually do like her, and she needs you. They all do."

Emeline laughed. "Your head's mince. I can't do anything but know what they're feel-ing. No one needs me sucking up their emotions like some leech."

"The shaman does." The goddess slapped at her sleeves before she gestured to the right. "You've left him all alone down there."

Turning her head, Emeline saw the beau-tiful blue and green sphere of the Earth floating against the black. "I can't be on the moon. There's no air, and it's too cold." She met Althea's gaze. "This is a trick."

"No, this is your mind," her friend corrected. "During the massacre you decided it was all too much for you. You've retreated so far into yourself that you might as well be on the moon. But you can't stay here, Emmie. You and Ruadri have more work to do."

Emeline stared at the Earth. For all the hell she'd been through, her lover had suffered just as much. More, considering the years he'd spent being battered by his father.

"Is he all right?"

"Not really. He's been trying everything he can to keep you alive, but, well, he's there, and you're here not wanting to go back. Frantic doesn't even begin to cover it." Althea came and gave her a somewhat dusty hug. "Ruadri needs to complete his task, Emmie, and he can't do that if you're gone. You have to do it together."

Emeline drew back. "He's been looking after me since I came to Dun Mor. He healed the affliction. He's protected me. He even tried to stop the *famhairean* from being created. I'm safe. What more do you want?"

"He wasn't supposed to save the Wood Dream, and that's all I can tell you. Sorry to play the goddess card, but it's all about the free will with you guys." Althea patted her cheek like a fond aunt. "It'll come to you. Just talk to him, which you also can't do from here."

"Wait." As the goddess began walking away, Emeline reached out, and saw her hand pass through Althea's back. "Please, I have to know more."

You love him, daughter of Seonag. 'Tis all he needs. Remember love.

The sky melted over Emeline, swaddling her in twinkling black velvet. Something tried to take Ruadri's tartan from her, and she pulled it back.

"Emeline?"

She opened her eyes and saw the shaman hovering over her. He looked so grim she tried to give him a reassuring smile. The taste of bitter herbs in her mouth instead made her grimace.

"Drink." He put his arm around her shoulders and held a cup to her lips. As she sipped some very cold water, he said, "I dosed you with a fever potion."

"It's terrible." As she drank more to wash away the taste, Emeline glanced up at the underside of a thatched roof, and the chinked stone walls supporting it. She smelled woodsmoke, and saw a fire burning in a small stone hearth. "Where are we?"

"A shepherd's shelter in the highlands." He helped her sit up and brushed the damp hair away from her face. "'Tis night."

Naked except for the tartan she still

clutched, she sat atop a pile of sodden fleeces.
A pot half-filled with water sat beside him,
into which he dropped a dripping rag. He'd
been bathing her to cool down her body, she
guessed, and wondered just how high her fever
had spiked. She pressed the back of her hand
to her brow, which was only a little warm.

"You fainted in the altar grove," Ruadri
said. "After that the *famhairean*...defeated the
Romans. Hendry and Murdina came and took
control of them. 'Tis done now."

Whatever he wasn't telling her must have
been horrible enough to drive her into
catatonia.

"The Wood Dream enchanted the totems
to come to life if they were attacked," she said.
When he nodded she felt sick. "Ru, why would
such gentle people create such monsters?"

"'Twas no' entirely their doing." Ruadri
then told her how the tribe had carved their
totems from sacred oak, which they enchanted
to guard the settlement. In the glen the giants
had encountered the rampant magic of the
unfinished solstice ritual, which gave them
more power. Absorbing the druids' souls had
somehow changed them from bespelled

objects to living beings. "'Twas said the Wood
Dream could speak with trees and regarded
them as part of the tribe. I reckon Hendry
and Murdina used that bond to bring the
famhairean under their sway. I failed."

His conclusions made sense but Emeline
had the uneasy feeling they had missed something important. "No, you didn't. The moon
told me that you weren't supposed to save
the tribe."

Ruadri frowned. "You had a vision
of her?"

Emeline told him of her strange encounter
with Meribeth and the goddess version of
Althea. "In the end she wouldn't tell me what
we're supposed to do. She wants us to figure it
out on our own. What else will happen in
this time?"

"Too much to fathom when you should be
slumbering." He kissed the top of her head. "I
shall fetch some dry fleeces from the shearing
shed."

Watching him go, Emeline felt the dull
brown boulders of his disappointment piling
inside her. She hated their failure to save the
druids just as much, but she'd never endured

the grinding weight of the burdens that Ruadri carried.

Or maybe I have, and I simply didn't realize it until it was gone.

The shaman had healed more than her affliction by bringing her to this time. He'd wanted her just as she was, with so much hunger and intensity that she might have been the sexiest female of all time. He'd treated her like a rare gift instead of a sorry joke of a virgin. He'd made her his lover, as if no other female had ever mattered to him. He'd freed her from all the self-loathing that she'd felt, and shown her the real woman she could be. He made her feel beautiful. He might not be in love with her, but because of him she knew she'd always feel loved. She also knew that before her no one had ever loved him for the man he was.

Tonight, that changed.

Emeline removed the tartan, shivering a bit as she went to kneel before the little hearth. The light from the flames danced over her pale body as she shook back and smoothed her hair. She expected the gnaw of doubt's persistent, chomping teeth, and slapped it away. While she might not have but one night of experience, she'd certainly watched enough films to know what being alluring was. Using her power for the first time on herself, she infused all the love she felt for Ruadri into herself, and watched the marks of the moon take on a rosy golden glow.

Ruadri came in carrying an armful of fleece, some of which he dropped as he caught sight of her.

"Emeline?"

"We've had a terrible day," she told him softly. "We've earned a wonderful night."

Letting her lips curve, she crooked her finger at him.

The rest of the fleeces fell on the others as the shaman approached her. She caught his hands and drew him down to kneel before her, and ran her fingertips down his neck and over his shoulders.

"You said there was so much more to this, and I want to learn," she murmured as she found the edge of his tunic, and drew it up over his head. Exposing the wall of golden muscle made her lips tingle, and she pressed a line of kisses from his collarbone to his flat nipple. "I loved it when you did this to me."

He groaned as she sucked on him until he puckered against her tongue. "We shouldnae. Your fever may return."

"Do I feel as if I'm burning up?" She brought his hand up to her breast and rubbed his palm in a circle over her mound. "That's because I am, for you."

Chapter Twenty

SLIPPING HER HANDS behind Ruadri, Emeline tugged on the laces of his trousers until they loosened. Easing him onto his back made her silently give thanks for the arms that lifting so many patients had made strong. Straddling him like a brazen besom proved much easier.

"You're mine, Shaman." She smiled down at him. "I've the marks to prove it. So when I want you, I should have you."

"Aye." Ruadri's gaze darkened as it shifted over her, and filled her with the hard, gleaming edges of his wanting. "So you mean to do as you wish with me."

"I do." Emeline bent down to press her lips to his, kissing him slowly and deeply. "I can't stop myself. I have to touch you." She shifted down to his thighs, rubbing her hands all over the tightening bulges and curves of his torso. "The way it feels when your skin slides against mine puts satin to shame. I wish I could wear you instead of clothes."

Doubt tried to bite her again as she began tugging down his trousers, but covering his belly with more kisses chased it away. When she turned around to work off his boots, she arched her hips so he could see all the curves of her bottom. Slipping his trousers off made her stretch down, and she let the tight peaks of her breasts graze over his knees. As she drew back up she caressed his long, powerful legs, admiring the heavy contours of the muscle and sinew that made them so strong. Atlas, who the Greeks thought had been condemned to hold up the weight of the sky forever, could not have had more beautiful legs.

"All mine," she murmured. "I can hardly believe it."

"I shall convince you," Ruadri offered, starting to sit up.

"Stay there. This is my night to have you."

Emeline wanted to see all of him, so she stood and took him in. The mightiness of the warrior had been refined by his druid blood, turning a man who might have been a hulking brute into a masculine masterpiece. That such a superb being looked at her now as if she were just as magnificent obliterated every trace of doubt. "Where do I start?"

"Anywhere," he said, smiling up at her. "'Tis much of me to have. Too much, mayhap."

"Never. You're so grand I could just stare at you for the rest of the night," Emeline told him as she knelt between his knees and rested her hands on his thighs. "But the moon didn't choose me to be your admirer. I'm your mate, Ruadri. That means my body is yours to enjoy, and yours is mine."

She glided her hands up to the base of his straining erection, encircling it with her fingers. Here he was primal male, full and thick and throbbing, hard as stone, smooth as polished wood. The distended veins and swollen head made evident his lust, but the subtle curve of his shaft made her feel acutely the emptiness between her thighs. They had been made to lock together, to give to and take from each other. When they did, they solved the ultimate puzzle of man and woman.

Ruadri reached down to pull back her hair, but otherwise watched her in silence now. She glanced up to see his expression shifting between soft wonder and hard need.

The molten gold wildfire of his arousal blazed through Emeline as she bent to kiss a bead of his cream, set like a pearl in the eye of his cock. The taste of him proved just as fiery-sweet as his scent, and ignited an edgy curiosity in her. She parted her lips to draw him into her mouth.

"Lass." He breathed out the word on a deep groan.

Emeline sucked gently, exploring all the shapes and textures of him. What she'd heard other nurses bemoan as a tiresome chore was nothing like that at all. She pleasured him with the glide of her tongue and the tug of her mouth, and through her ability knew it made him ache to thrust deeper. No magic could have put him under her spell like this.

Having such a hold over him brought with it a sense of power that immediately became addictive. How much of him could she take? Did the sight of his cock in her mouth please him as much as her licking and sucking? Would she make him come this way? It excited her to think of him jerking under her as she swallowed each jet, if she could do that for him. He was so big, and her mouth so small.

"Emeline, please." He shook now as his thighs tensed, and the heavy sac of his balls tightened under her palm. "'Tis too good."

He'd never done this with a woman, either, Emeline sensed, and that decided the matter. She wrapped her fingers around his shaft, sucking steadily on as much as she could take, and working her hand up and down on the rest. Sounds of her own delight came up to hum against his cock, which twitched and swelled in response.

She knew the moment before he came, feeling it in the explosions of heat and light inside her and the surging tremors that poured up through his shaft. She drank him down as easily as she'd sucked him, every pulse of his seed warming her mouth and throat as she swallowed.

Gently Emeline released him and crawled up to lay on his chest. The staccato thrum of his heartbeat applauded her, and the sheen of his sweat soothed her heated face.

"That was lovely," she murmured.

Ruadri folded his arms over her. "You didnae need do such for my pleasure."

"Maybe I needed that for mine." She raised her head and rested her chin on her hands. "You didn't like it?" The look he gave her made her blush. "If I was clumsy I'll keep practicing until I get better. I want to be a good lover."

He touched her mouth, studying it before he met her gaze. "'Tis no' about facking, this bond between us. To look upon you brings me joy. You need never bed me for it."

"I don't have to do anything. I want you. I love you." The moon had been right about that, she thought as she kissed his fingers. "And you can't say that you're unloved anymore, because I'll never stop."

He gripped the hair at the back of her head. "You do this for me, when I've said naught a word of love to you."

Emeline shrugged. "It's not about words.

I've tried to love my parents, my work, my patients, and even a friend that I knew didn't care for me. I don't regret it, but love can't happen when it's one-sided. So you don't have to tell me anything. I know what you feel for me. Every time you touch me you tell me."

"I said naught because I reckoned you'd think me mad." He brought her hand to his mouth, opening it so he could kiss her palm. "I saw you first in a dream, and in it I ran to you, Emeline. I didnae think or consider or hold back my heart. I ran to you no' because I dreamt you mine, but that you've always been my dream."

In her mind snapshots of her outside the wedding shop flashed, showing this time the shaman trying to save her. "Oh, Ruadri. You were there that day?"

"In spirit, aye, and I've longed for you every moment since. In that dream I fell in love with you, my beautiful lady." He sat up with her and tipped up her chin. "I loved you before I saw you in truth. I've loved you each moment since. I'll love you until I'm no more." He touched his brow to hers. "Wife."

No wedding vows could have been lovelier

than his promises, and Ruadri sealed them with a kiss as he lifted her in his powerful arms. He carried her over to the pile of fleeces he'd dropped. He kept kissing her as he used his foot to spread them out, and then lowered her onto their fluffy softness.

Emeline hardly had time to catch her breath before Ruadri parted her thighs and lifted her legs over his shoulders. His mouth found her swollen and slick, and then he pushed his tongue into her. As his lip grazed her pearl he penetrated her over and over, pressing as deeply as he could. Now she lay at his mercy, and whimpered and writhed as he laved her with hungry strokes of his ravishing tongue.

Seeing his face between her legs and feeling the brute force of his need as he made love to her with his mouth drove Emeline from shocked arousal to flooding pleasure. When the sensual storm broke inside her, he drew back and pinned her down, guiding his cock-head to her spasming pussy.

"Wife," he said again, grunting as he plowed into her.

His ravenous need and relentless shaft

fucked her to a second climax, one that made her body bow beneath him. He swallowed her cries before he pushed a hand under her and lifted her breasts to his mouth. His teeth grazed her pulsing nipples as he sucked each one. Clamping his hand around the curves of one mound, he pressed his fingers into her, weighing her, playing with her.

Emeline pushed her breast against his tongue, her whole body thrumming with the jolts of his plunging cock. Now she had to take instead of give, and she took every inch he pumped into her, hard and thick and demanding her surrender. His feelings saturated her with his earthy lust, the rampant need to invade her body like an earthquake destroying everything in its path. He needed her to come apart for him, to give her body as completely as her heart.

Emeline wrapped her legs around him and clamped down on him, gripping him as she exploded again. He held her and watched her and fucked her, and only when she gasped out the last of her breath did his shoulders shake and his cock go impossibly deep. She felt him jerk over her and inside her as his seed shot again and again into her clenching softness.

Ruadri rolled over, holding her pressed to him, and let his head fall back as he splayed his hand over her buttocks. "I shallnae ask forgiveness for that, my lady."

"You didn't do anything wrong. Which should make me suspicious now that I think about it." Emeline turned her head to kiss his chest and sighed. "Are you sure they kept you in chains every time?"

His deep chuckle shook her. "Aye, 'twas the practice, I promise you." He threaded his fingers through her hair before he paused and went still. "When this is done, will you go back to your time?"

She thought of the work-filled, lonely life she had led as a nurse. "My family's all gone. There are plenty of people to take my place at the hospital. I've nothing else to go back to." She lifted her head. "Isn't it strange that we're all like that? I think all five of us are unmarried, childless orphans, with only our work filling our lives in the future."

"When Brennus becomes confounded he

says he feels the hand of the Gods at work," Ruadri said, smiling. "Will you stay?"

Emeline didn't hesitate. "Yes, I will. But in which time?"

"Here, until we learn how to return to mine." He groaned as she lifted herself from him and reached for his tartan. "In the morning we'll seek shelter in the highlands with Ara's tribe. That should give us more time to reckon."

"All the Romans are dead now," she said as she shook out the tartan and used it to cover both of them as she lay back down. "Ara's tribe is safe."

"I think no', lass," Ruadri said. "Two *centuriae* attacked the Wood Dream, with but one hundred sixty soldiers. They came from a legion that numbers in many thousands. When they dinnae return, more shall be sent in search of them. They'll no' find their bodies."

Emeline remembered feeling the first Roman being devoured a moment before she blacked out. While the horror of it still scarred her heart, she wouldn't retreat from it again.

"I know what happened to the soldiers,

Ru. What will the Romans do when they can't find the missing *centuriae*?"

He pulled her closer, warming her with his body heat. "Raid every Pritani village in this territory to search them. They'll torture the tribes until they tell them what they wish to ken. As only we saw what happened in the glen, many shall die."

She thought of the little girl she had kept from sliding into the stream. "Maybe we should convince Ara to move his tribe to another part of Scotland, to be safer." She felt him stiffen and looked up at him. "What is it?"

"When we arrived here, Drest said he didnae ken the name of my clan. Nor did Ara." Ruadri stared at her as if he'd never seen her before now. "Emeline, your tribe hasnae made their pact with Brennus."

Emeline listened as he told her of the bargain made between Ara's tribe and the Skaraven in return for defending them against the invaders, which in twelve centuries would lead to the alliance of the clan with the McAra, but she still couldn't make the connection.

"What happens if they don't make this pact with your clan?"

"The Romans shall find them, and the tribe has no chance of surviving the fury of the legion," Ruadri said, his voice bleak. "'Twill alter history. Ara shallnae found the bloodline of the McAra."

She went still as the implication sank in. If Ara and his tribe were killed, then every one of their descendants would never be born. Thousands of people would never be born.

"That's why we were brought back to this time."

"'Twas to save your bloodline," Ruadri said, and kissed her brow. "To save you, Emeline."

"Then the solution is very simple," she said firmly. "We find Ara and tell him what happened in the glen. We convince him to make the pact with your chieftain."

"Ara never summoned Brennus." His voice went flat. "'Twas my sire, Galan. I always wondered why he had intervened. In this time, he lives in seclusion, and doesnae have any dealings with the Pritani."

"Ruadri, everything we do here now has

already happened, and we're the only ones in this time who know what will happen." She bit her lip. "It has to be you who persuades him to send for your clan."

"Aye." He met her gaze. "But 'tis no one Galan despises or wishes to suffer more than me."

Chapter Twenty-One

I NSIDE THE TULLACHS' cottage, Brennus warily accepted some hot brew from the headman's wife. "My thanks, Mistress."

Cadeyrn stopped his inspection of the cozy front room and shifted slightly to eye the contents of the mug.

"'Tis no' poisoned," the old druidess advised him drily before she regarded her mate. Fingal sat speaking in low tones with Bhaltair but looked up when she called his name. "The chieftain and his second await your counsel, Husband. Since their clan awaits them, and feel no fondness for druid kind, I should hurry things along."

Bhaltair exchanged a look with Fingal

before he said, "From what you've said, Chieftain, we think my acolyte Oriana lured you to the inn."

Brennus came to stand by the table, and deliberately took a drink from the mug before setting it down. "That young lass who blames the Skaraven for her grandfather's killing?"

The old druid nodded, and related her disappearance and the grim items found in her belongings. "The lass has a powerful ability to commune with the dead. 'Tis possible through her gift she has been brought under the sway of Barra Omey, a bone-conjurer seeking vengeance on me."

"Barra may yet live," Fingal added. "By now she would be too old to act herself."

"Alive or dead, 'twould be a canny move to use the lass," Cadeyrn said. "None would suspect an untrained druidess capable of slaying a chieftain."

Brennus's patience was thinning. "So, this Barra seeks vengeance by sending Oriana to burn me and blame you for it. What did you do to her?"

"I dinnae ken," Bhaltair said. "I never crossed paths with Barra Omey, nor was I part of the conclave that judged her. Of course, we shall make inquiries of the archivists—"

Brennus made a cutting gesture. "What of Ruadri and the McAra healer?" At the druid's blank stare, he added, "They've gone from Dun Mor. Did you lure Ruadri somewhere with the promise of healing her?"

"'Tis the first I've heard of them missing." Bhaltair looked genuinely shocked now. "In her condition 'twould be too dangerous to move her. Had I some aid or cure to offer, I'd send it to Ruadri."

Cadeyrn studied the old druid's features a moment longer before he murmured, "Truth."

"Mayhap he took her through…but what can I ken of it," Bhaltair added quickly. "He doesnae, ah, confide in me."

Brennus didn't need his war master to read the druid's deception. "Lie again to me, old man, and I shall gut you."

He raised a gnarled hand to his brow before meeting the chieftain's gaze. "'Tis likely the lad brought the lady to a sacred grove. Taking her through would heal her affliction."

"As it did Lily's broken neck," Cadeyrn

said, nodding. "But Emeline wasnae in any state to open the portal for our shaman."

"She didnae have to. Ruadri's druid kind." Under their stares Bhaltair seemed to shrink. "'Twas Galan who sired the lad in secret. After his Pritani mother died in childbirth, he treated him very harshly. Galan also used the threat of killing all the Skaraven to compel the lad to watch and report on your clan during your mortal lives. Had I been aware, I assure you, I'd have put an end to it."

Brennus's temper was close to boiling over, but forced it back by recalling how faithfully Ruadri had served the clan—every hour of both his lives. Whatever he had been made to do, he knew the fault lay with the druids.

"I shall deal with my shaman when we find him. Because of you, we face a clan war with Maddock McAra." Brennus glowered at Bhaltair. "You'll be the remedy."

Instead of blustering the old man nodded and rose to his feet. "I put myself wholly in your hands, Chieftain. However I may aid you, 'twill be done."

"I think that unwise," Fingal said at once. "Oriana wishes you both dead, and when she learns she has failed she shall try again. Chieftain, Bhaltair isnae a warrior like you. He will be safer with us."

Cora came and rested her hand on his shoulder. "One cannae hide from evil, Husband. 'Tis our duty to fight it."

"No harm shall come to Flen from me or mine," Brennus told the headman. "More than that I cannae vow."

The old druid eyed Fingal. "I maynae be a warrior, old friend, but I'm no' helpless."

"Nor we." Fingal glanced up at his wife before he said, "The Sky Thatch shall take up the search for Oriana, and call on our neighboring tribes to aid us. When she's found, she'll be placed under spell guard and held until her master returns to decide on her fate."

Bhaltair murmured his thanks before he regarded the chieftain. "What would you have me do?"

"Ride with us to the McAra stronghold, and act as negotiator," Brennus said. "Tell Maddock all that you ken, and forge a truce until we find your acolyte and my healers."

Cora made a concerned sound. "You think

it wise, Chieftain, to reveal so much to your mortal allies?"

"'Tis that, Mistress, or clan war." He nodded to her and her husband, and then left the cottage with Cadeyrn to retrieve their mounts.

"Say what you will of the tree-knowers," his war master mused as they entered the druids' stables. "They've curious troubles and mountains of secrets."

"Aye, bone-conjurers and vengeance schemes," Brennus muttered as he stalked to the stalls. "And Ruadri born druid kind. Next, we shall be invaded by the Finfolk, and told they sired the rest of the clan."

"I doubt it. No' one of us sports gills." His war master went into one stall and came out again. "Flen spoke another truth. His pony's no' fit to ride."

"'Tis why I shall need another mount," Bhaltair said as he joined them, and leaned over the stall door to give the pony a fond stroke. "Chieftain, I'm in no place to ask for your mercy, but I would just the same."

Brennus already knew what he wanted. "I shallnae kill your lass for setting me to burn."

He turned around to meet the old meddler's gaze. "As you willnae end her for wishing vengeance on you."

Bhaltair looked relieved rather than offended, and nodded before he said, "If 'tis Barra who uses Oriana, then you need ken more of her powers." He glanced at Cadeyrn. "And plan how we may fight them."

"We fight. You keep out of it." Shoving a saddle in the old druid's arms gave Brennus a small amount of pleasure.

Once they left the settlement and rejoined the waiting Skaraven, Cadeyrn rode a little ahead of the clan with Brennus, and said, "You cannae kill one druid for what another did, Bren."

"'Tis memory that plagues me. Recall how often Ru returned bloody and bruised after training alone with Galan? Near every time. I saw how he looked at that brutal bastart, but told myself 'twas just an echo of my own resentment." He shook his head. "Why didnae he tell me of this, Cade?"

"As Flen said, to keep the rest of us alive." His war master's jaw tightened. "After what they did to us, likely he hates himself even more than his sire despises him."

Bhaltair trotted his gelding up between them. "I dinnae crave to further rile you, Chieftain, but you must ken what Barra did, and what she may do through Oriana."

Brennus slowed his mount. As much as he despised the old druid, his acolyte had come close to ending him. "Regale us," he said sourly.

"Barra Omey's transgressions compelled the conclave to outlaw all bone-conjuring fifty years past." He grimaced. "'Twas an ancient practice of bringing back the dead, frowned on even then. Out of respect for the disincarnated, 'twas rarely attempted."

Cadeyrn gave the old druid a skeptical look. "You raised us from our graves."

"'Twas a different matter, War Master," Bhaltair countered. "Bone-conjurers used their magics to invite the souls of the dead to speak to them. They bespelled the bones left behind to summon their spirits. Only Barra didnae wait for the living to die. She sacrificed them."

Disgust filled Brennus. "She killed so that she might speak to their spirits?"

"Worse, I fear. After a sacrificial ritual, Barra tore the newly-dead souls from their afterlife. She attempted to force them back into their own corpses." He cleared his throat. "'Twas no' made known at the time of her judgment, but she had managed to resurrect a few mortals."

"You did as much with us," Brennus said. "What of it?"

"We transformed you into immortals," the old druid corrected. "Barra didnae ken or didnae care to revive the flesh. The bodies of the souls she trapped kept rotting. In the end the conclave freed the imprisoned by burning them."

"By the Gods," the war master muttered, shaking his head.

After being nearly burned alive himself, that settled the matter for Brennus. "If this Barra yet lives, ken that I shallnae spare her."

"You'll no' need to," Bhaltair assured him, his querulous voice now flat and cold.

Halfway to the McAra's stronghold Brennus

called a halt, and directed the clan to ride to the loch and return to Dun Mor. The men didn't look happy as they left them, nor did it please him to approach the castle without his brothers at his back. Yet if the Skaraven arrived as a warband, that was how Maddock would treat them.

"I'd send you along with them," he told Cadeyrn, "but I need your owl inside the stronghold."

His war master simply nodded. His ability to spot weakness in anything allowed him to detect anything from falsehoods to an opponent's most vulnerable position on the battlefield.

When Brennus saw the first of the laird's patrols he sheathed his sword and dismounted. Cadeyrn did the same before he helped Bhaltair to the ground. A few moments later six large McAra clansmen approached them, blades held ready.

"Skaraven arenae welcome here, Chieftain," Maddock's tall, burly second-in-command said, but slowly lowered his sword. "My sentries saw you send away your warband. Do they await with our sister?"

Brennus shook his head. "We come to

warn your lord of a new enemy, and in hopes of calling a brief truce." He unbuckled his belt and offered it and his sword to the tanist. "We dinnae wish a war with your clan."

The big man's gaze narrowed before he accepted the weapon. "A truce would be most welcome, Chieftain."

After collecting Cadeyrn's blade the McAra clansmen flanked them on all sides and marched them to the stronghold. As they walked Brennus noted the large number of guards posted along the outer curtain walls, and lookouts high above them on the tower walks. No doubt every other McAra male who could hold a blade watched them from places of concealment, ready to defend their laird and his family.

That 'tis come to this, Brennus thought as he stopped a short distance from the gatehouse. *All for a squabble over a sick lass.*

The tanist disappeared inside for a few minutes before he returned and dismissed his men. "The laird grants you a brief visit, that you may assure we've well-treated your weapons master."

That was Maddock's slap back at his intentions, Brennus thought, but nodded.

Inside the stronghold's great hall more armed men had gathered, positioned at every entry and standing ready. The laird himself looked remarkably unconcerned as he sat by the hearth reading and sipping wine from an ornate goblet.

"The scroll he reads," Cadeyrn murmured, only loud enough for Brennus to hear. "'Tis blank."

Maddock leisurely looked over at them. "I've sent for Kanyth Skaraven. He shall be delivered from the dungeons–" He paused as his steward hurried over and whispered something to him. Then he scowled. "Gods damn me. Who let him out this time?"

The pale-faced steward grimaced. "I believe 'twas your lady wife, my lord."

"I should have wed McFarlan's horse-faced sister." Maddock crumpled the blank scroll and tossed it into the hearth. "Why do you yet stand there?" he said to the steward, and motioned for him to leave. "Go fetch our hostage, that his kin may inspect him."

Kanyth appeared a few minutes later,

escorted not by guards but most of Maddock's children. From the look of the wooden swords and pillows the lads carried they had been playing at battle. Their sisters wore circlets woven of straw and brightly-colored ribbons, and fluttered kerchiefs like so many fine ladies.

The laird rose to his feet and regarded his family with a narrow gaze. "Now 'tis no' the time for frolic."

"'Twas my fault, my lord," Kanyth said. "I should have remained in my cell. Forgive me." He pulled off the lad clinging to his back and handed him to the laird's wife. "'Tis good to see you, Chieftain, War Master." He frowned a little at Bhaltair. "And druid I reckoned to be dead."

Before anyone could speak the laird's youngest daughter rushed over to Maddock. "Father, my brothers routed Ka five times at battle, and killed him thrice, and he a Skaraven."

"Indeed." The laird's lips twitched before he leveled a stern look at his lady. "I recall we agreed to keep the prisoner in the dungeon."

"So we did, my love. Our bairns, however, didnae," his wife said, and curtseyed to Brennus. "Despite his many losses I think your brother an excellent sparring master, Chieftain. Come now, my dear ones. 'Tis time for your lessons." Over the groans of her children Lady McAra herded them out of the great hall.

Maddock watched them go, and then turned to face Brennus. "Dinnae mistake my misplaced affection for my younglings as pardon for what you've done."

"Never," Brennus said. "With your leave, I would speak to Kanyth while the druid relates to you some news."

The laird looked suspicious, but after a moment nodded his consent. As the druid went to speak to him Kanyth joined Brennus and Cadeyrn.

"Yesterday Maddock arranged a betrothal between McFarlan's son and Emeline to better secure their alliance," the weapons master said. "Dinnae bring her here unless she wishes to wed." He eyed Brennus's tunic and his grin vanished. "You've been burnt."

"More than once." He quickly related the attempt on his life in Aviemore, and the disappearances of the healers and the acolyte.

"Whatever truce Flen manages to arrange, you must remain here to protect the laird and his family."

"This while I'm their hostage." Kanyth's brows arched. "A true challenge."

Chapter Twenty-Two

AT SUNRISE RUADRI left Emeline sleeping and went to check on their mounts. The horses remained in a nearby sheep pen where he had left them last night, and both whickered a greeting. He fetched water for them from the shelter's well, and then checked their hooves. As he left them to graze a little longer, he spied a large patch of purple and red wild raspberries where the trees edged the grasses.

Emeline shall love those.

Picking the fruit also gave him time to think of how he would approach his sire. After finishing Ruadri's training Galan had promised never again to come within sight of him. To approach him would doubtless seem like a deliberate attempt to provoke him, especially as he now lived in one of the most secretive and closely-guarded settlements in Scotland.

Likewise, Ruadri didn't want to go anywhere near Galan. He also couldn't allow his sire to discover that he had mated with Emeline, or why they needed him to send for the Skaraven. If he knew, Galan would refuse to help them.

Ruadri's heart still grew tight as he walked back to the shelter. There he smelled the scent of porridge cooking and ducked his head as he stepped through the low threshold.

"Good morning," Emeline said and came from the hearth, a spoon in one hand, and stood on her toes to kiss him. "I rummaged about and found a sack of oats and some cooking things. We'll have some porridge in a few minutes."

He eyed the pot she had hung on the hearth hook. "You ken how to cook."

"Not as well as Lily, but I manage. You should see what I can do with chestnuts and an old Roman shield. Oh, raspberries," she said as he unwrapped the heap he had picked. "They're better than bananas."

They had to eat directly from the pot, sharing the one spoon she'd found. As they broke their fast Emeline tried to explain to him what a banana was. She blushed a little when she described its shape and size, which sounded remarkably like a man's penis.

"So, you cut them up to put atop your porridge," Ruadri said, and glanced down at his lap. "Mayhap I should keep from the kitchens, lest my manhood be mistaken for this fruit."

"Oh you're much larger than a banana," Emeline told him, and then groaned and covered her eyes. "I can't believe I fell for that."

He suddenly understood why she made so merry: to keep him from thinking about his sire and the difficult task they faced. But time was not on their side. Feeding her the last berry, he kissed her lips.

"'Tis a long ride to the Moss Dapple settlement. We must go."

She curled her hand around the back of his neck. "I'd do this for you if I could."

Together they tidied the shelter. Ruadri left one of the protective amulets he carried by the sack of oats, as payment for what they had used. "When we reach my sire's settlement, you mustnae tell my sire we're mated. Show me no affection and say as little as you may. The less Galan kens, the less he can use as a weapon."

"I'll be careful." Emeline touched his cheek. "You didn't kill your mother, Ru. You were just a helpless newborn. She died because it was her time. If you could ask her, do you think she would blame you for her death?"

Thanks to Galan's hatred he'd spent his life carrying the weight of his mother's death inside. He'd never once considered what Fiana might have felt.

"I cannae tell you."

"I think she'd tell you that any mother would gladly give her life so her child could live," Emeline told him, and took his hand in hers.

Together they retrieved their mounts, and rode from the highlands toward the Moss Dapple's settlement. With each league they crossed Ruadri's determination grew stronger. As a lad he had feared Galan's cold brutality, and as a man he'd despised his sire for forcing him to turn traitor. The druid's hatred for him would always be a threat, but Ruadri wouldn't live imprisoned or humiliated by it anymore.

"I owe you much, Wife," he told Emeline when they stopped at a stream to water and graze the horses. "You see everything with such clarity of heart."

"That's more Cade's gift, I think. I see you." She embraced him before she drew back. "I just wish everyone knew what a rat your father is."

"Aye." That gave Ruadri more to think on, and he began to plan.

As they rode he talked with her about how to handle Galan. The sun dipped low by the time they reached the river entrance to the Moss Dapple's enchanted forest. Ruadri stopped and eyed the waterfall, knowing Galan's defenders had already spotted them. Once they dismounted he tethered their horses and kept his empty hands where they could be seen.

"I would have you remain here," he said. "'Twould be safer."

"The moon said we have to do this together," Emeline countered. "Your strength and my gift combined. It's a good plan, my love."

Ruadri took in a deep breath. If they were killed, they would go to the well of stars together. So, no matter what the outcome, they would be together.

"Stay ever at my side," he said lowly.

Leading her into the river, they walked through the water illusion until they reached the thundering falls that guarded the only entry to the forest. Ruadri glanced at his lady, who nodded slightly before she walked into the cascade beside him.

Ruadri saw the shapes of men waiting ahead, but no one entered to confront them. He shifted in front of Emeline as they walked, grateful for once for his own massive body, which served as an excellent shield. When they reached the end of the passage he stepped out into the dimming sunlight.

Five bare-chested druids as large as himself surrounded them, but instead of the defenders' traditional scythes they held swords. The intricate skinwork inked on their bodies resembled nothing Ruadri had ever before seen.

"You trespass, Pritani," the largest of the defenders told him.

"No, Domnall. Like you, he hunts."

A towering black-haired druid emerged from the trees. Wearing dark green robes worked with glyphs made of twigs and leaves, and holding a silver sword worked with black stones, Galan looked just as grim and forbidding as Ruadri remembered.

"Sire." He bowed to his father.

Galan regarded Emeline for a long moment before he met Ruadri's gaze. "You force me break my vow, Shaman. Have you forgot yours to me?"

How like Galan to refuse to say his name. "I would ask a word alone with you, Sire," he said evenly. "A Pritani tribe in peril needs help."

"You come to beg a boon from me." Galan laughed, making a dry, rusty sound as if he hadn't done so in years. "'Tis why you brought the wench? As a bribe, that I may forget what you be?"

A warm, loving sensation passed over and around Ruadri, steadying him enough to answer civilly. "Mistress Emeline belongs to the tribe in danger."

"Aye, but she be a cursed halfling like you." Galan bared his teeth in an unpleasant smile. "Who do you put in chains when you fack?"

Emeline stepped between them. "Invaders come hunting my people," she said, her voice low and respectful. "I ask you summon the Skaraven chieftain to meet with my tribe, that they may bargain for their protection."

Ruadri could feel Emeline pouring her calming radiance over Galan. He also saw the tell-tale shimmer of his sire's body wards as they repelled her magic.

"My son's hoor seeks to enchant me while she spouts lies." The big druid's glittering eyes shifted to Ruadri. "Why cannae you summon Brennus?" When he didn't reply Galan turned his back on him and said, "Take their heads, Overseer."

Domnall didn't move. "Mistress, what tribe?"

"The Ara," Emeline said. "They fled to

the highlands but shall soon return to their village. They cannae prevail alone over the Romans."

"Domnall," Galan grated. "You serve me, no' this wench. Kill them now, else they bespell us all."

The overseer gave the big druid a long look before he planted his sword in the ground at Ruadri's feet. "There be no quarrel here but of blood," he told Galan. "You wish your son dead, *Dru-wid*, so you must end him."

"*No*," Emeline cried out.

"Mistress," Domnall cautioned her as he put a hand on her arm. "No interference. I cannae permit it."

"Keep your pathetic enchantments to yourself, you hoor," Galan spat.

"Keep her safe," Ruadri said to Domnall. He pulled the blade from the earth before addressing his sire. "What need you of body wards, my brave Father? I remember you always said that I made a poor swordsman." He gestured to himself. "Yet I wear none. 'Tis fear of me that keeps you cloaked?"

"There's naught I fear less than a mewling

welp," Galan snarled and made a show of dropping his wards.

Ruadri grinned. "Mayhap if you hadnae beat my arms with your cudgel before blade training, I'd have improved."

The druid's face contorted, and he rushed at him with a roar of outrage.

Ruadri parried Galan's first savage blow with a shaking arm and stumbling feet. "I've no more talent for crippling or killing than I had as a lad." He ducked to avoid a sweep of his sire's blade. "'Twas why you set a warband to kill me, and watched me defend myself alone."

"Silence," his father shouted, and slashed the front of Ruadri's tunic, spilling first blood.

"Ruadri," Emeline shrieked as she struggled against Domnall's grip. "Let me go!"

"Keep her back!" Ruadri shouted, barely dodging Galan's thrust.

A sly look crept over Galan's twisted face, his eyes darting back and forth between his son and Emeline.

"More than a hoor, I'd wager," the older druid said. "Look at her. The wench 'tis crazed with worry." He smiled wickedly. "And the way you look at her." He nodded in Emeline's direction. "You've taken a mate. How I shall enjoy hacking you to pieces before her."

Again and again his sire attacked, driving him back into the tunnel and toward the falls. Ruadri continued to call out memories from his boyhood exposing Galan's cruelty, all the while handling his own sword with clumsiness. As he expected, the druid lowered his guard after inflicting dozens of minor wounds.

When Ruadri felt the falls at his back, he glanced past Galan's shoulder to see Emeline rushing toward them as Domnall staggered back. He then employed his true skill and struck, slashing his father's forearm from wrist to elbow, and knocking his blade into the water illusion.

Seizing Galan by the front of his robe, Ruadri pinned him against the side of the tunnel. "Now, we shall have our word alone."

"You never said anything about a duel," Emeline gasped as she joined them.

"'Twas easier to fight than talk." Looking at his struggling sire, he said, "Your son yet dwells with the Skaraven, so I cannae summon them. The Gods sent me back in time to assure you do it."

Galan's eyes widened. "You came from time henceforward."

"Aye, and 'twould please me to stay and tell your tribe of every wrong you did me." He watched fear fill his sire's eyes, but took no joy in it. "You shall summon my clan to help the Ara as we've asked. If you refuse, I'll go to Bhaltair Flen and tell him all. He'll have you removed as headman and brought before the conclave for judgment. You ken what they'll do to you."

Galan stopped writhing and sagged. "I'll send for your wretched clan." As Emeline came closer he lifted his head and his lips peeled back from his teeth. "Dinnae try your soul-sharing on me again."

"It's not as bad as you think," she said, a terrible pity in her eyes now. "I know you're upset by this, but we'll be returning to our time. You'll never see us again."

Ruadri saw confusion replace his anger as Emeline's influence changed his emotions.

"Come with me to the dovecote," Galan muttered.

When they emerged from the tunnel, Domnall rushed over to them as Emeline held up a hand.

"My apologies, Overseer," she said quickly. "My fear overwhelmed me. 'Twas never my purpose to share it with you."

Though his angry expression said otherwise, he nodded his grudging assent to her.

Ruadri handed the bloodied sword back to Domnall. "My thanks. We've made peace, and now go to send a summons for the Skaraven."

"Aye, and then you'll go," the overseer said, glancing at Emeline. He made a gesture that sent his men ahead of them.

Emeline kept focused on Galan and poured her magic into him. The headman trudged along willingly as they made their way to the settlement. In the small round house where the tribe's messenger birds were kept, Ruadri wrote the summons himself on a tiny scroll. After attaching it to the dove Galan selected, he released it, and watched until the bird flew out of sight.

"We shall leave now by your sacred grove," he told his sire, who stared back at him with dull eyes. "My thanks, Sire."

"Fack you and your hoor," Galan muttered.

"His own feelings are fighting mine, and mine are losing." Emeline gave Ruadri a pained look. "We'd better hurry."

Domnall escorted them to the sacred grove, where he regarded them both for a long moment. "Our headman shall punish me for my meddling, but 'twas worth it. No Pritani should endure without their tribe."

"Nor druid kind." Ruadri clasped arms with him. "Many thanks, Overseer."

After Domnall left them Emeline stepped into the circle of stones with Ruadri, and held his hand tightly. "What if it doesn't open this time?"

"Then we go to our mounts and ride away fast." He drew their joined hands down to the grass and touched the earth with them.

Slowly the soil whirled open into a dark, spinning vortex, and Emeline heaved a sigh of relief.

"Thank heavens," she said, and turned her head to look back at the settlement. Her back stiffened, and she lunged in front of him.

A thudding sound made Ruadri go still,

until Emeline began to slide down his front. He caught her, and then saw the arrow shaft protruding from her chest. He jerked his head up to see Galan standing at the edge of the oak grove, notching another arrow on his longbow. Their eyes met, and Ruadri saw such gloating in his sire's gaze that he nearly ran at him. Then his lips moved, and while no sound came to his ears, he knew exactly what Galan had said.

A wife for a wife.

"No, Ru." Emeline uttered a liquid cough. "Home. Please."

A second arrow sliced across Ruadri's upper arm as he lifted her up, but he felt nothing. All he could do was look down at his lady's still face. He could feel her blood soaking through her garments, and the warmth of her body ebbing. When a third arrow struck him in the thigh, he came out of his daze.

Holding Emeline close, Ruadri leapt into the portal.

Chapter Twenty-Three

✦

BEING CARRIED IN Ruadri's strong arms helped Emeline endure the hard, deep pain spreading through her chest. She couldn't take a deep breath, and wondered if one of her lungs had collapsed. Then the world spun away into darkness, and her body filled with light.

This time, however, it couldn't heal her completely, because the arrow still remained embedded in her chest. It stuck out from the exact spot where her heart still beat. From the way it quivered, her heart had healed around it.

Snow fell on her cheeks and brow, and spangled her eyelashes. She could see the thin white clouds of Ruadri's breath puffing out over her. They'd traded summer for winter, but Emeline didn't mind. The frigid air felt just as good as the pale sunlight. She didn't resent the huge white snow drifts her lover trampled through as he carried her from the hidden grove. She might never have worn a wedding dress, but she'd loved, and had a husband, and she hadn't winked out of existence.

Because of her and Ruadri, her bloodline was safe again.

The arrow in her chest, on the other hand, presented a problem that couldn't be solved. She had spent too many years in the medical field to overestimate her chances. Even with emergency open-heart surgery she'd likely die. And since Ruadri was carrying her into Dun Mor now, that wasn't going to happen. She understood the protector mark now, though. Somehow the moon had known what she would do to save her lover. It had been complete instinct.

"We're home, my sweet lady," Ruadri said.

As men shouted and a woman shrieked, she peered up at him. He looked terrible, covered in her blood, his handsome face almost as gray as his eyes. She glanced down and saw a bent arrow sticking out of his leg where it had healed inside the wound. He'd have to cut that out, and it would hurt like the devil. She wished she could stay long enough to help him, but her time with him was rapidly coming to an end.

Emeline saw the quivering of the arrow slowing as Ruadri lowered her to his work table, and gathered the dregs of her strength.

"What happened?" That was Rowan. "Where have you been? Emeline, are you all right?"

The carpenter loomed over her, furious until she saw the arrow. Then she dropped out of sight, and a man who looked like an angel picked her up and carried her out.

Rowan is fainting, and I'm seeing angels. That's not good. Or maybe it is.

Lily came next with Althea, and their husbands, and their low voices whispered around her. Everyone was afraid, and that was something Emeline could do something about, even with an arrow in her heart. She adored these brave women, and their heroic men. This clan, her family. She sent that love out into all of them, taking away their sorrow and replacing it with joy.

The effort made her tired, but she couldn't sleep, not yet. She looked at her beloved shaman.

"Ru. I'll come back."

Her lover stopped what he was doing and leaned down to kiss her brow. "You mustnae go. I'll take you through the portal again. I've but to cut out the shaft—"

"Can't. It's inside my heart. I can't survive you removing it." She managed to put her hand on his arm. "Be back someday. Wait for me?"

"Oh, Gods." His tears fell, warm and soft, on her nose and cheeks. "I'll wait, and I'll love you. Until I'm no more, Wife."

That would give her plenty to dream of in the next place, Emeline thought, and smiled. What did the druids call the afterlife? *The well of stars.* She liked that even more than heaven.

"Husband."

She was glad she'd said that. It would be her last word, and she wanted it to be the best, brightest, most beautiful thing she'd ever said.

That he was.

Ruadri knelt beside the table, still holding her hands, and lay his head on her belly. Behind him a white, glowing sphere rose and hovered over them both. Before Emeline closed her eyes, she saw a face looking down at her from inside the moon. This time it wasn't Althea's. In fact, she'd never seen such a beautiful woman, and then realized she was looking at a face very much like her own. Maybe Ara's tribe wasn't the beginning of her bloodline after all. Maybe it went back long before druids and mortals.

Didn't matter, really. A huge rush of emotion poured through Emeline, and wrapped her in the shining snowy silks of moonlight. *Thank you, Goddess.*

Remember love, my daughter.

❧

RUADRI FELT Emeline's last heartbeat, and heard the breath sigh from her lungs for the final time. He knew what he had to do, but he stayed where he was, holding onto her even after she had gone. His love, his protector. His wife, who had sacrificed herself for him.

Standing and pulling the arrow out of his thigh barely dented his grief, but he had more precious work to do. He cleaned his wound blade, and used it to gently remove the arrowhead piercing her still heart. Tossing it away, he stitched together the edges of the wound, and then washed away the blood from her skin. His own pattered onto the floor, making it slippery until he poured water over the deep puncture, and it healed.

"Shaman."

He looked up to see Taran on the other side of the table. Everyone else had left, probably when Emeline had died. He couldn't think of how long ago that had been.

"You must tell them now."

The keeper of the clan's secrets, Taran had likely always known what he was.

When Ruadri did that, he could be with Emeline again. "Gather the clan in the great hall."

The horse master nodded and left.

Ruadri wrapped his wife in his tartan, smoothing her dark hair over the folds before he carried her out into the hall. There he placed her on the fur by the hearth, and stood over her as the Skaraven assembled around him.

Althea came and held out a silver chain to him. "Kanyth finished this for you." Tears streamed down her cheeks as she looked at his wife. "He said it was for Emmie." She choked back a sob as he took it. "I thought she… should have it." The lairds wife covered her mouth with both hands as she wept.

Ruadri fumbled with the delicate catch for a moment, and then bent and clasped it around his wife's throat. Looking down at her peaceful countenance gave him the courage to straighten and face his clan.

"I thought myself unloved until Emeline came to us," he said. "'Twas wrong of me. All of you have loved me as a brother. For that you deserve the truth."

He could hear the flatness in his voice as he related their journey through time. He was unmoved as he described how they had failed to save the Wood Dream but kept the tribe of Ara from being killed by the Romans. Brennus and Cade exchanged a surprised look when Ruadri spoke of compelling Galan to send the summons to them that led to the pact between the two clans. No one moved when he told them how his sire had tried to kill him at the portal, and how Emeline had shielded him to die in his place.

Finally, he confessed that he not only had been sired by Galan but had kept his druid blood a secret. He also detailed the reports he had given to the druids, and how he had been trained as a weapon of last resort. As he spoke of his betrayal, he looked directly at Brennus, who showed no emotion in response.

"Galan made me offer myself to the moon, in hopes I would be given the gift of her light," Ruadri told the chieftain. "Had the Skaraven ever attempted to harm the innocent in our mortal life, I was to use my blinding power on the clan." He looked around the hall at the shocked faces watching him. "I've been a traitor since boyhood. 'Tis how I returned your affection and brotherhood, with deceit and lies. For that I no longer deserve to be one of the Skaraven." He removed his clan ring and handed it to Brennus. "I'm ready to die. I would ask that Cadeyrn take my life."

He knelt before the chieftain but looked over at Emeline. In a few moments he would return to the well of stars, where she awaited. That was all he had left. That was all he needed.

"War Master, counsel," Brennus said.

His second came to join him, and both men regarded Ruadri for a long silent moment.

"'Twas good of Ru to enlighten us," the chieftain said. "But he didnae speak the complete truth, and that muddles my thinking."

"Aye." Cadeyrn stroked his chin. "No' a mention of Galan's threats to kill us as lads if he didnae serve as Watcher."

"The scheme to blind us, should we turn to evil," Kelturan put in. "That curdled my cream." When the other men glared at him, he shrugged. "What if he mistook some mischief for evil? A man shouldnae have his eyes burnt out of his head for shouting and kicking some pots."

Ruadri was completely drained as he looked up at Brennus. "Please, Chieftain. I shall beg your forgiveness as much as you wish, but 'tis done now. I wish only to be with my lady."

"Aye, but hold your blade, War Master," Brennus said as he walked over to Emeline's body. He knelt beside it as he unclasped the chain, and slid Ruadri's clan ring onto it.

Silvery white light glowed around the black ring, turning it silver. The glow expanded, and then burst out in a huge wave of magic. The force blasted tables and benches against the walls, and knocked over every Skaraven.

Ruadri pushed himself up from the stone floor to see Brennus helping Emeline to her feet. His lady looked bewildered but otherwise unharmed, and then saw him and ran. He staggered to his feet in time to catch her in his arms. He felt her warmth and softness and still could not believe it.

"Did I keep you waiting long?" Emeline asked, and snuggled against him.

Over her head he stared at the chieftain. "I spied on you. I betrayed you. I'm druid kind."

"Half-druid," Brennus corrected. "Had you been all druid, I might have ended you. But all that you did protected the clan. That and you cannot choose your sire, nor those in which you must confide."

"I heard that." A very wet and bedraggled Bhaltair Flen appeared and made straight for the hearth. "'Twas all my doing, lad. I made the mistake of revealing the truth of your past to Brennus. He knew all long before you returned to Dun Mor."

"But you swore to keep my secrets," Ruadri said faintly.

The chieftain snorted. "That he never does."

"That pledge but slipped my mind. Be happy you shall never grow old," the druid told him, and squeezed the hem of his robe into an ash bucket. "Lady Althea, may I trouble you for some dry garments to borrow until my own dry? Unless you favor the great puddles I shall make in your hall."

Brennus came over to rest his hand on Ruadri's shoulder. "We've much to tell you, now that you're come home." To Emeline he said, "I'm happy to welcome you as my shaman's wife. Maddock McAra, however, wishes to inspect you with his own eyes, and I cannae predict how he shall take the news. Mayhap you and Ru shall help me convince him no' to chop off my brother Kanyth's head."

"I'd be happy to talk to my laird, Chieftain," she said, smiling. "I'd like to tell him about Ara and his tribe. They were marvelous people."

As the clan began setting the great hall to rights, Ruadri slipped into his work chamber with Emeline. There he kissed her until they both lost their breath and laughed between gasps.

"'Tis as if I've been given a third life," he told her as he stroked his hand over her dark hair. "One I wish to spend loving you and serving my clan. 'Tis what you want as well, Emeline?"

"I do." She touched the clan ring hanging on her chain. "Forever."

Chapter Twenty-Four

✦❧✦

SOME DAYS LATER Maddock McAra entered his bed chamber to see his wife sitting by the window and unbraiding her fine hair. The moonlight caught some of the new silver threads in the long tresses, but he secretly thought they made her look even more beautiful. Even after all these years together the fact that she had accepted his hand still astonished him, something he also concealed.

"Again, pursuing your idle pleasures, Elspeth." He came over and took charge of her plaits, gently releasing them into rippling waves. "Now that our guests have left, I reckon we have the place to ourselves again. The mad druids and the *famhairean* have vanished, mayhap for good, along with that acolyte of Flen's. We've naught to worry on for at least fourday. Shall I chase you in your night rail through the halls?"

"With half our clan yet under our roof?" She shook her head. "You must confine your pursuit of me to the solar or our chambers." She caught his hand and drew it down to her belly. "Until spring comes, when I shall be obliged to waddle, and become too simple to catch."

"A new bairn," he whispered. A smug happiness filled Maddock as he splayed his fingers over the gentle curve. "I thought as much. You've been aglow of late." He pressed a kiss to his favorite spot on her long, lovely neck. "This one shall be your image."

Elspeth chuckled. "Aye, if my hair turns black and my eyes blue, like Emeline."

He picked her up and took her to his great chair, where they talked of the pleasures to come. He adored his children, and worshipped his wife for her gentle patience with their ever-growing brood. Maddock was surprised, however, when his lady asked if she could be attended during her confinement by their new kinswoman, Emeline.

"You'll have all that you wish, except that cheese you favored with young Duncan," Maddock said. "The smell of it near killed me. But why would you wish Lady Emeline to tend to you? You ken more about birthing than a midwife proper."

"I'm not a young lass anymore, Husband, and it would comfort me to depend on such a learned lady." She glanced at him. "You're no still annoyed that she wedded the Skaraven shaman. No' after what they did for our bloodline."

He fiddled with the lace at her wrist as he struggled with his pride. "I'm the McAra, Ellie. 'Twould have been pleasant to be consulted."

"But now we've a kinship tie with the Skaraven," she pointed out. "No other clan in Scotland can claim such a bond."

"Truth." He sighed. "Comforting, too. Long after we're gone Ruadri and Emeline shall yet remain. As kin they'll always look after our clan. 'Tis fortunate as well that I

agreed to the truce. Ending Kanyth Skaraven
wouldnae have improved on the matter."

"You forget what Lady Emeline said,"
Elspeth said, smiling at him. "Mayhap we'll
return to look after the McAra as the new
laird and lady."

"So the Gods would curse me to live this
life again. Very well, we shall have fourteen
bairns in the next." He kissed the tip of her
nose. "Come to bed. I wish to fondle your
pretty belly."

A soft knock came on the door, and a
young face peeked inside. "Forgive me, my
lady, but you sent for me?" the maid asked in a
broad lowland accent.

"Ana, yes, please come in. The laundress
delivered the wrong bed linens to our room."
Elspeth climbed out of her husband's lap and
went to the big armoire in the corner of their
chamber. "Maddock, this is our new chamber
maid, Ana Breem."

He inspected the lass, who had hair the
color of brambleberries and placid dark eyes.
"Serve your lady well, young Ana, and I shall
be very pleased."

As his wife instructed the servant on which

bed linens to remove and place in their guest rooms, Maddock turned down the coverlet and went into his dressing room to change into his night shirt. It would come off along with Ellie's night rail as soon as the maid left them, but appearances had to be kept.

"'Twill be done as you wish, my lady," Ana said when he returned, and bobbed to him before carrying out a large stack of linens.

"How did you find a lowlander, and why do we need another maid?" Maddock asked as he undressed his wife.

"She came looking for work." Elspeth smothered a yawn. "Poor lass lost her only kin to the *famhairean*. I thought it a kindness."

"You're too generous," he scolded her as he climbed into bed with her. "Next you'll be collecting kittens from the barns and owlets from the rafters."

"We must do what we can, Husband." She pressed his hand to her belly. "And she shall help much when the new bairn comes."

❧

OUTSIDE THE LAIRD's bed chamber, the chambermaid stood listening until the voices fell silent. She carried the linens to the nearest guest room, where she dropped them on the floor and flopped on the big bed.

It vexed her still not to know where Bhaltair Flen had fled. She knew it could not be Dun Mor, for the Skaraven chieftain despised the old bastart too much to offer him sanctuary. Still, she expected she would find him as she continued her search for the Skaraven.

As Ana Breem she would work hard to make herself necessary to Lady Elspeth and invite her confidence. All mortal females of high rank told everything to their servants, and even the laird might speak unguarded in her presence. What she couldn't learn from the lady she'd glean from eavesdropping. Being kin to the Skaraven meant the McAras would know much she could use.

Aside from losing track of the old druid, Oriana was quite pleased with herself. She had positioned herself in the perfect place to learn the location of Dun Mor. Once she had it, she would at last take revenge for her murdered love.

It would be glorious, and soon.

THE END

• • • • •

Another Immortal Highlander awaits you in Kanyth (Immortal Highlander Book 4).

For a sneak peek, turn the page.

Sneak Peek

Kanyth (Immortal Highlander, Clan Skaraven Book 4)

Excerpt

CHAPTER ONE

THE FIRE HAD gone out again. No wonder Perrin Thomas's hands and feet had turned into lumps of ice. Even before she'd been starved half to death she'd always gotten chilled easily. In her own time, she would have had central heat, an electric blanket, cuddly pajamas and fuzzy socks to keep her warm. Here in the fourteenth century she had a scratchy wool blanket, borrowed clothes that felt like burlap, and an ancient fireplace that wouldn't stay lit.

Rowan would know how to build a fire with two rocks and some twigs. And keep it burning. In her sleep.

Perrin had always depended on her strong, capable younger sister to handle any sort of trouble, but she couldn't do that anymore. She'd told Rowan she could take care of herself. Here in the subterranean refuge of Dun Mor, the hidden stronghold of the Skaraven Clan, she was on her own.

"I can do this," she muttered as she pushed herself out of bed. She yelped as a sharp piece of straw poked up through the ticking and scratched her backside. Jolting to her feet, she turned and swatted the mattress. *"Stop attacking me."*

Outside in the hall heavy footsteps thudded, and the door to her chamber burst open. The big, dark-haired man who came in held a longsword only slightly less intimidating than the fury in his black eyes. The tightly-muscled wall of his bare chest heaved as he scanned the room, and then regarded her.

"Who dares harm you, my lady?" Kanyth Skaraven demanded.

"It's the bed." She hated how whispery and helpless her voice sounded, but with all that man-chest in her face she could hardly breathe. Ever since she'd come here she'd been fascinated by the weapons master—so much so that she kept having erotic dreams about him. "Uh, the stuffing stabbed me."

"Indeed." Slowly the clan's weapons master lowered his blade as he peered at her. "Show me this wound."

"That's okay. I'm fine." She took a step back. "You can go back to, ah, whatever you were doing."

"Brennus sent me to guard you," Kanyth said as he sheathed his blade and loomed over her. His powerful body heat enveloped her trembling form in an invisible embrace. "Show me where you're hurt, lass, that I may comfort you."

Unfortunately, nothing about the big man made that possible. Up close he smelled of hot cinnamon and cloves, as if he sweated spices. She'd never seen such a perfect face on a guy, as though he'd been laser-sculpted

from some flawless marble. His hair fascinated her, like some mass of polished onyx
mysteriously spun into midnight threads. A
faint blue light glowed along the lines of the
primitive tattoos on his chest. Perrin felt
herself swaying toward him and stumbled
back another step.

"I'm comfortable," she said, her voice
tight. She gulped as he put his big, scarred
hands on her shoulders. Now he was touching
her, and she shook so hard she'd probably
break into a million pieces. "Really, I am."

"I think no'," Kanyth murmured. "You've
naught but yourself here...and me." He
moved one palm down the length of her back,
and then cupped the stinging curve of her
scratched buttock.

"Um, okay," she managed to whisper. The
sensual caress made her skin heat up until she
thought she'd combust. But wait. What was
that sound? Was she moaning? "Please, what
are you doing?"

"All that you secretly desire," Kanyth
crooned as he leaned down, touching his lean
cheek to hers. "For you're my wench."

Wench.

He kept saying that but he began shaking her.

Wench.

"If you dinnae awake, wench," a much deeper, annoyed voice said, "I'll call the shaman to pour one of his wretched potions down your gullet."

Perrin's eyes flew open to see a brightly-burning fireplace, a bowl of porridge under her nose and a frowning rugged face hovering over her. It took a moment before she realized she'd dozed off again.

"Yes? I mean, yes. I'm comfortable. I mean, very cozy." Ignoring whatever was still stabbing her in the butt, she beamed at the Scotsman. "I'm fine."

"Oh, aye, for a hank of hair and bones," Kelturan said. The Skaraven's chief cook, fussed with the wool blanket covering her legs before he pushed the bowl into her hands. "Eat, or I shall toss you in my pottage kettle."

She nodded and even took a spoonful to satisfy the grouchy cook, although it tasted like lumpy paste. Once he trudged back to the kitchens she glanced around to see if anyone in the great hall was watching her. Dozens of big Skaraven warriors sat quietly eating around the enormous table shared by the clan for meals. Armed sentries occupied positions by every entrance, their eyes watchful. Three more towering men stood listening to Brennus, their chieftain, who appeared to be issuing orders.

Perrin set aside the porridge and started to relax until she saw the silhouette of the man standing by the back wall, the one who looked like a polished, refined version of the chieftain. He had the same glittering black eyes, and he was definitely watching her, but not in a protective, I'm-guarding-you way. No, Kanyth Skaraven always looked at her as if she were an uninteresting child. Which, considering the fact that he was an immortal highland warrior with some sort of scary superpower no one talked about, seemed apt.

Oh, God, had she been talking in her sleep? What if he'd heard her? Or everyone had? She'd die of embarrassment. Just die.

Her face flooded with painful heat as she ducked her head and reached under her hip. She pulled out Emeline McAra's wooden knitting needles, and what appeared to be a scarf the nurse had been knitting. She hadn't looked in the chair when she'd come up from her room and sat down by the fire to warm her frozen feet. At least that explained part of the dream.

Perrin tried to eat a little more of the pasty porridge, but the familiar morning headache began to pound inside her skull. Absently she rubbed her temple, wishing she could get over the caffeine withdrawal. She'd always needed at least two cups to wake up properly, but the nearest Starbucks was seven hundred years away. Of all the reasons that tempted her to go back, vanilla latte sat at the top of the list.

"What ails you, my lady?"

Perrin froze and looked up into narrowed black eyes. She had to say something to Kanyth or he'd make a fuss. Then everyone would come over and she'd be the center of attention. Again.

"Nothing," she lied.

The weapons master crouched down to her eye level. "Lady Althea told us you've visions of what shall come. Have they again begun?"

Of course, her former ability to see things

in the future would be the only reason Kanyth spoke to her. But the visions hadn't come since Lily had conked her on the head to keep her from doing something brave and stupid. She should tell him that her ability would probably never work again. But no, instead she sat like a silent lump in front of the man, who looked even more gorgeous close up. Too close for Perrin's personal space issues, her shyness locked up her throat and threw away the key.

He scowled. "Shall I summon Ruadri?"

Perrin would talk to Kanyth, right now, because this was ridiculous. She took in a deep, slow breath as she tried to calm down. She should have gotten over this exasperating anxiety years ago. A grown woman who had survived being yanked back in time by crazy magic people and their horrible abuse and weeks of starvation should be able to speak a couple of words. Especially to one of the nice men who protected her now. Only he was leaning in now, and she'd squeak or stutter or make him believe she was even more of a nitwit than he thought.

She cringed back and shook her head.

Kanyth stood, looking as frustrated as she

felt. "Mayhap you'd feel easier with one of the ladies."

I'd feel better if you held my hand and waited and let me breathe through this, Perrin thought. *Then maybe I'd tell you that I want to do something to help find the mad druids. I know how much you and the clan need to stop them, and make sure they can never hurt anyone again. Or maybe I'd tell you that I've been dreaming about you every time I close my eyes. And that's really scaring me, because maybe the visions have come back, but as dreams, and you're part of them. Or maybe I'd say that somehow I'm meant to be with you. But that would mean you'd have to want me instead of looking at me like a boring kid.*

All she could do was shake her head again.

• • • • •

Buy *Kanyth (Immortal Highlander, Clan Skaraven Book 4)*

DO ME A FAVOR?

You can make a big difference.

Reviews are the most powerful tools I have when it comes to getting attention for my books. Much as I'd like it, I don't have the financial muscle of a New York publisher. I can't take out full page ads in the newspaper— not yet, anyway.

But I do have something much more powerful. It's something that those publishers would kill for: **a committed and loyal group of readers.**

Honest reviews of my books help bring them to the attention of other readers. If you've enjoyed this book I would so appreciate it if you could spend a few minutes leaving a review—any length you like.

Thank you so much!

MORE BOOKS BY HH

For a complete, up-to-date book list, visit
HazelHunter.com/books.

Get notifications of new releases and special
promotions by joining my newsletter!

Glossary

Here are some brief definitions to help you navigate the medieval world of the Immortal Highlanders.

acolyte - novice druid in training
Am Monadh Ruadh - the original Scots Gaelic name for the Cairngorm mountains, which translates to English as "the red hills"
apoplexy, apoplectic - medieval terms for "stroke" and "suffering from a stroke"
arse - British slang for "ass"
aye - yes
bairn - child
baggie – Scottish slang for "big-bellied"
banger – Scottish slang for "penis"
barmy – British slang for "crazy"

bastart - bastard

bausy – Scottish slang for something large, fat and coarse

baws - balls, testicles

beastly - British slang for something horrible or arduous

Beinn Nibheis – old Scots Gaelic for Ben Nevis, the highest mountain in Scotland

besom – Scottish slang for a promiscuous woman

besotted - British slang for strongly infatuated

bhean – Scots gaelic for "wife"

black affronted – very embarrassed, extremely humiliated

blaeberry - European fruit that resembles the American blueberry

bleeding - British obscenity, roughly equivalent to "damned" but much more offensive in the UK

blethering – Scottish slang for talking a lot without making much sense

bloke - British slang for a male

blethering - chatting

bleezin' -drunk

blind - cover device

blood kin - genetic relatives

bloody - British obscenity, see bleeding

boabie – Scottish slang for "penis"

bone-conjurer – a druid who uses the bones of the dead to communicate with their spirits

boon - gift or favor

boyo - British slang for a boy or man

Bràithrean an fhithich - Brethren of the raven

braw - Scottish slang for "outstanding"

brieve - a writ

brilliant - British slang for excellent or marvelous

broch – an ancient round hollow-walled structure found only in Scotland

buckler - shield

bugger - British slang for a contemptible person

caber tosser – an athlete in a traditional Scottish field event who throws a large wooden pole called a caber

cac - Scots gaelic for "shit"

caibeal - Scots Gaelic for "chapel"

cairn - a pile or stack of stones

Caledonia - ancient Scotland

cannae - can't

caraidean - Scots Gaelic for "friends"

centuria – (plural centuriae) a Roman legion
detachment of eighty men

chap - British slang for a male

cheeky - British slang for slightly disrespectful

Chieftain - the head of a specific Pritani tribe

chuffie – Scottish slang for fat-faced, portly

chundering - British slang for throwing up

clodhoppers - British slang for work boots

clout - strike

cocked up - British slang for something done
very badly

coddle - pamper

codswallop - British slang for "nonsense"

comely - attractive

conclave - druid ruling body

conclavist - member of the druid ruling body

confinement (relating to pregnancy) – childbirth

cosh - British slang for "hit"

couldnae - couldn't

cow - derogatory term for woman

croft - small rented farm

cross - British slang for "angry"

cudgel - wooden club

daft - crazy; Scottish slang for "unstable"

death oan a prin stick – "death on a prin

stick"; Scottish slang for someone who looks deathly sick

demi - French term for a half-size bottle of champagne; holds 375 ml

dinnae - don't

disincarnate - commit suicide

doesnae - doesn't

dru-wid - Proto Celtic word; an early form of "druid"

eagalsloc - synonym for "oubliette"; coined from Scots Gaelic for "fear" and "pit"; an inescapable hole or cell where prisoners are left to die

ducat - a gold European trade coin

ell - ancient unit of length measurement, equal to approximately 18 inches

epicure - a person who takes particular interest and/or pleasure in gourmet dining and drinking

fack - fuck

facking - fucking

famhair - Scots Gaelic for giant (plural, famhairean)

fathom - understand

feart - Scottish or Irish for afraid

Finfolk – Scottish mythological equivalent of mermen and mermaids

firesteel - a piece of metal used with flint to create sparks for fire-making

flat – apartment

fortlet - a little fort

fortnight - British slang for a two-week period of time

Francia - France

Francian - French

funeral pyre – the pile of wood on which a corpse is burned

Gaul - ancient region that included France, Belgium, southern Netherlands, southwestern Germany, and northern Italy

Germania - Germany

girthie – Scottish slang for fat or heavy

goosed - Scottish slang for "smashed"

gormless - British slang for someone with an acute lack of common sense

gowk – Scottish slang for "simpleton"

granary - a storehouse for threshed grain

greyling - species of freshwater fish in the salmon family

hasnae - hasn't

hauchan – Scottish slang for a lump of mucus one coughs up

Hispania - Roman name for the Iberian peninsula (modern day Portugal and Spain)

hobble – to tie or strap to keep something from straying; usually a horse

huddy – stupid

incarnation - one of the many lifetimes of a druid

isnae - isn't

jobby - Scottish slang for "shit"

joint salve – topical rub for sore or stiff joints

jolly good - British slang for "excellent"

keeker - black eye

ken - know

kip - British slang for "nap"

knackered - British slang for exhausted

lad - boy

laird - lord

land of the white bear - the Arctic

larder - pantry

lardy cake – a rich dessert cake or bread made with lard, spices, currants or raisins

lass - girl

league - distance measure of approximately three miles

leannan - Scots Gaelic for "beloved"

lochan - a small lakelot - British slang for a group, usually made up of people

maidenhood – virginity

magic folk - druids

make a hash of it - British slang, to do something badly

manky - British slang for "disgusting"

mate (nickname) - British slang for "friend"

máthair – Scots Gaelic for "mother"

mayhap - maybe

mind-move - telekinesis

minging - stinky

mojo - American slang for "magic"

mòran taing - Scots Gaelic for "many thanks"

morion - a brown or black variety of quartz

mustnae - must not

naught - nothing

night rail – a loose robe worn as a nightgown

no' - not

nod off - British slang for going to sleep

NOSAS - North of Scotland Archaeology Society

nutjob - American slang for a crazy or foolish person

nutter - British slang for a mentally-disturbed person

on about - British slang for "talking about"

on the mooch - Scottish slang for spying on someone á la a Peeping Tom

oubliette - a dungeon with an opening only at the top

ovate - Celtic priest or natural philosopher

pike - pole

plonker - British slang for "idiot"

podgy – chubby

prattling - to talk for a long time on inconsequential matters

Pritani - Britons (one of the people of southern Britain before or during Roman times)

quim - medieval slang for the female genitals

reeks like an alky's carpet - very smelly

ruddy - a British intensifier and euphemism for bloody

scarper - British slang for "run away"

schiltron - a medieval battle formation used to form a living barrier or wall of troops

scullery - a small back room off the kitchen where the dishes or laundry are washed scunner - Scottish slang for an object or person that causes dislike and/or nausea

sett – the burrow that a badger digs

shag - British slang for sexual intercourse

shambles - British slang for an extensive or serious mess

shambolic - British slang for "chaotic"

sheshey – Scots Gaelic for "husband"

shite - British slang for "shit"

shouldnae - shouldn't

side ladders - the slatted upper sides on the back of a medieval cart or wagon

skelf – Scottish slang for wood-splinter thin

skellum – Scottish slang for rogue or scoundrel

skelp - Scottish slang for slap, hit or beat

slee - sly, cunning

Sluath – mythic air-riding demonic immortals who steal the souls of vulnerable or dying mortals

snaiking – Scottish slang for "sneaking"

sod (verb) - British slang for "screw"

sod all - British slang for "nothing"

solar - rooms in a medieval castle that served as the family's private living and sleeping quarters

solicitor - British term for lawyer

soul-sharing – druid term for empathy

speak-seer - a druid who can communicate with the dead and channel their voices

spew - vomit

staunch weed - yarrow

stone (weight) - British weight measurement equal to 14 lbs.

stone lifter – someone who dead-lifts heavy ancient stones kept in various places in Scotland

swaddled – tightly-wrapped in linen to prevent movement, used on infants

tanist – the rank name for a Scottish laird's second in command

Tha mi a 'gealltainn - Scots Gaelic for "I promise"

'tis - it is

'tisnt - it isn't

tor - large, freestanding rock outcrop

tree-knower - the Skaraven nickname for the druids of their time

thick with - closely involved, relating to "thick as thieves"

transom - a weight-bearing support crossbar

trencher - wooden platter for food

trews - trousers

'twas - it was

'twere - it was

'twill - it will

'twould - it would

uisge beatha - old Scots Gaelic for "whiskey"

unbodying – removing a *famhair's* spirit from his physical form

undercroft - a room in a lower level of a castle used for storage

vole - small rodent related to the mouse

wallapers – Scottish slang for "idiots"

wanker - British slang for a useless person

wasnae - wasn't

watchlight - a term for a grease-soaked rush stalk, used as a candle in medieval times

wazzock - British slang for "idiot"

wee - small

wench - girl or young woman

whidder – Scottish slang for forcing someone to do something

willnae - will not

wouldnae - would not

Yank - UK slang for "American"

your head's mince – Scottish slang for "you're deeply confused"

Pronunciation Guide

A selection of the more challenging words in the Immortal Highlander, Clan Skaraven series.

Ailpin - ALE-pin
Althea Jarden - al-THEE-ah JAR-den
Am Monadh Ruadh - im monih ROOig
Ana Breem - AH-nuh BREEM
Aon - OOH-wen
apoplexy - APP-ah-plecks-ee
Ara Alba - AIR-ah AL-bah
Aviemore - AH-vee-more
Barra Omey - BAH-rah OH-mee
Beinn Nibheis - ben NIH-vis
besom - BIZ-um
Bhaltair Flen - BAHL-ter Flen

bhean - VAN

Black Cuillin - COO-lin

Bràithrean an fhithich - BRAH-ren ahn
EE-och

Brennus Skaraven - BREN-ess skah-RAY-ven

Bridei - BREE-dye

broch - BROCK

caibeal - KYB-al

cac - kak

Caderyn - KAY-den

cairn - KAYRN

Cailean Lusk - KAH-len Luhsk

caraidean - KAH-rah-deen

Cenel - SEN-ell

Coig - COH-egg

Cora Tullach - CORE-ah TULL-luck

death oan a pirn stick - deth ohn a peern stik

Dha - GAH

Domnall - DON-uhl

Drest mag Ara - DRESSED MAWG AIR-ah

eagalsloc - EHK-al-slakh

Duncan - DUN-kin

Elspeth - EL-spehth

Emeline McAra - EM-mah-leen mac-CAR-ah

famhair - FAV-ihr

Ferath - FAIR-ahth

Fiana - fee-AHN-ah

Fingal Tullach - FEEN-gull TULL-luck

Galan - gal-AHN

Girom - JEYE-rum

Gwyn Embry - gah-WIN AHM-bree

Jared - JAIR-red

Hendry Greum - HEN-dree GREE-um

Kanyth - CAN-ith

Kelturan - KEL-tran

Lauren Reid - LOR-in READ

Liath - LEE-ehth

Lily Stover - LILL-ee STOW-ver

lochan - LOHK-an

Maddock McAra - MAH-duck mac-CAR-ah

Magda - MAHG-dah

Manath - MAN-ahth

Marga - MAR-gah

máthair - MAH-thur

McFarlan - mick-FAR-len

Meribeth Campbell - MARE-ee-beth CAM-bull

mòran taing - MAW-run TAH-eeng

Moray - MORE-ray

Murdina Stroud - mer-DEE-nah STROWD

Ochd - OHK

Oriana Embry - or-ree-ANN-ah AHM-bree

Perrin Thomas - PEAR-in TOM-us

Rowan Thomas - ROW-en TOM-us

Ruadri - roo-ah-DREE

schiltron - SKILL-trahn

Seonag - SHOW-nah

sheshey - SHEZ-eh

Sluath - SLEW-ahth

Taran - ter-RAN

Tha mi a 'gealltainn - HA mee a GYALL-ting

Tri - TREE

uisge beatha - OOSH-ka bah

whidder - WID-der

Dedication

For Mr. H.

Copyright